"You want a reason to hate me? How's this?"

Jarrod pulled her roughly against him. As if in a dream Brooke watched him as he slowly lowered his head, his mouth claiming hers in a kiss that was totally savage. He forced her lips apart, his arms like steel bands as she struggled to be free.

Against her will, Brooke found herself responding. This was incredible, she thought. Jarrod Stone was kissing her—and she loved it!

Suddenly she was no longer in his arms. "Get inside!" he ordered harshly. "I'll see you tomorrow."

Brooke made her way slowly up to her apartment, still dazed. Her burning anger had turned into something completely different. Instead of making her hate him, he had just confirmed the fact that she was in love with him!

Other titles by

CAROLE MORTIMER
IN HARLEQUIN PRESENTS

Many of these titles, and other titles in the Harlequin
Romance series, are available at your local
bookseller. For a free catalogue listing all available
Harlequin Presents and Harlequin Romances, send
your name and address to:

HARLEQUIN READER SERVICE,
M.P.O. Box 707,
Niagara Falls, N.Y. 14302

Canadian address:
Stratford, Ontario, Canada N5A 6W2

CAROLE MORTIMER

engaged to jarrod stone

Harlequin Books

TORONTO • LONDON • LOS ANGELES • AMSTERDAM
SYDNEY • HAMBURG • PARIS • STOCKHOLM • ATHENS • TOKYO

Harlequin Presents edition published October 1980
ISBN 0-373-10388-3

Original hardcover edition published in 1980
by Mills & Boon Limited

CHAPTER ONE

BROOKE SAT DOWN at the reception desk, turning to face the girl who sat behind her. "Has he arrived, yet?"

Jean gave her an innocent look. "Has who arrived?"

Brooke gave her an impatient glance. "You know very well who. Don't tease this morning, Jean."

Her friend quirked one eyebrow. "Had one of those nights, did you?"

"Morning actually. *Has* he arrived?"

"I gather you mean Mr. Stone? Then yes, he arrived about ten minutes ago."

"Oh, damn," Brooke frowned her displeasure.

"Why? Did you want to see him?"

"Not really." She pursed her lips. "I...he...what did he look like?" She watched the other girl closely.

Jean gave her a strange look, dealing hurriedly with a call that came through on her switchboard. They weren't due to open until nine o'clock, and yet invariably there were calls coming through before then. "How do you think he looked?" she said finally. "How does he always look—gorgeous; just as tall, dark, and handsome as usual."

"He didn't look...well, different?"

Jean gave a firm shake of her head. "He always looks the same, he always acts the same. He walks in here, gives me an arrogant nod of his head, and then walks straight into his private elevator. He does the same thing in the evenings only in reverse. The man's as impersonal to his employees as the machines he produces. Three years I've worked here now, and he still wouldn't recognize me if he saw me out in the street."

Their conversation was broken off as the office workers started to crowd into the building in preparation for starting work at nine. As the receptionist, Brooke found the next half an hour very busy, directing people up to the various offices and dealing with the loudspeaker system.

The morning rush over, she relaxed in her chair for a few minutes. Jean was kept busy with her switchboard, which gave Brooke time to think. She was a fool, a prize idiot. She was likely to lose her job for what she had done, and it was a good job paying a very high salary.

She must have been temporarily insane—must have had a brainstorm. When she had seen the announcement in the newspaper this morning she had felt sick, physically sick. And yet no one else had seen it, at least, no one had commented on it. Someone had to see it soon, it was so noticeable. It had seemed larger than life to her.

It had been there in the newspaper for all to see, an intended marriage between Brooke Faulkner and Jarrod Stone. Her own engagement to the owner of this prosperous computer firm! And to make matters worse, he knew nothing about it!

She picked up the internal telephone on her desk as it began to ring. "Brooke Faulkner speaking," she said automatically.

"Get up here!" snapped a deep male voice.

She almost dropped the telephone in her panic. Jarrod Stone, it had to be! She cleared her throat. "I...I beg your pardon?"

"You'll do more than that when I've finished with you," he growled. "I'll expect you in my office in precisely five minutes." The receiver was slammed down at the other end.

She didn't need to be told that he knew about the announcement in the newspaper, the anger in his voice had been enough. Besides, he had hardly ever spoken to her before, there could be only one reason he wanted to see her.

"Everything all right?" Jean asked, noting her pale face.

Brooke realized with a start that she was still holding the receiver in her hand. She put it hurriedly back on its cradle. "I...I have to go up to one of the offices. Would you...would you look after the desk for me for a while?"

"Sure," Jean agreed readily.

Brooke didn't quite know how she got into the private elevator for the tenth floor, but somehow she seemed to have managed it. She had only ever used this elevator once before in the six months she had worked for Stone Computers, and that had been two weeks ago when she had been induced to seek this terrible revenge on him.

It had all started when the model had arrived to take the advertising photographs. No one else had been available to take her up to Jarrod Stone's office and so she had offered to take her up herself. It had been a good excuse to see him. As Jean had so rightly said, he walked in in the mornings and out again at night, taking no notice of them in reception at all.

As it had turned out Jarrod Stone's secretary had gone to lunch that day and her assistant was off sick. She had hardly been able to believe her luck when she had stepped out of the elevator into the outer office. The place had been deserted, which meant she would actually get to speak to Jarrod Stone herself. Since the day she had begun work here and he had walked into the building to begin his day's work, she had fallen for him—hard.

He was so fantastic looking, like a film star or something. He was tall, well over six feet, with a lithe athletic body that indicated he did not spend all of his time in an office, and his skin was tanned from much time spent in the sun. His dark overlong hair was styled away from his face, his deep gray eyes narrowed and enigmatic.

But if she had been instantly attracted to him he hadn't reacted at all to her, those gray eyes looking right through her. She knew she wasn't beautiful, but she wasn't that plain, either. Dark brown hair with deep red tints swung easily around her shoulders in gleaming waves; her deep blue eyes surrounded by long thick lashes, her small uptilted nose, curving mouth that was never far from a smile, and slight, slender figure all added up to an attractive young girl. And yet to Jarrod Stone she might not even have been feminine.

But she knew he wasn't always that reticent about noticing a woman's charms; he was reputed to have had many beautiful women in his life at one time or another. And his completely self-assured arrogance pointed to them not all being platonic relationships. No, here was a man who had shared his bed with many women—and he had known how to satisfy every one of them.

In a way it had been his confirmation of these conquests that had sparked off her desire to hit out at him. Leaving the model in the outer office she had passed through to the reception room. In here she could hear the faint murmur of masculine voices, and she had realized Jarrod Stone wasn't alone.

She soon knew the reason she could hear their voices, too; the office door was slightly ajar. She was just about to knock on the door when she was arrested in the action by the words being murmured in her boss's deep throaty voice, his amusement obvious.

"I'm afraid I only find women good for one thing," he scoffed lightly. "And I don't mean housework," he added with a laugh.

Brooke had stepped back with a gasp. What a cheek! What a nerve! The meaning behind his words had been obvious and she had waited open mouthed for his companion's answer. She knew she should really knock on the door and make them aware of her presence before they said anything else, but she was held mesmerized by the arrogance of the words she had just overheard.

"Come on now, Jarrod," the other man replied, this voice sounding younger. He had called the first speaker Jarrod, confirming her belief that Jarrod Stone had made that insulting remark about the female sex. "You like women as much as I do," he continued.

"I *enjoy* them," Jarrod Stone had corrected. "I don't know that I've ever actually liked them. But I've desired them, yes. But I find them preferable more as bed companions than as anything else."

"If one of them could hear the way you're talking...."

But one can, she wanted to shout. She had never felt so disgusted and degraded. How a man as successful and good-looking as Jarrod Stone, could judge all women by the type he had obviously been associating with for years was beyond her. To her he appeared the most handsome man she had ever seen, and to think he had that low opinion of women just didn't seem fair. His looks and charm had obviously done him no good whatsoever, making him cynical about women.

"Why should they care," he replied carelessly. "They are usually well compensated for their... charms, for want of a better word," he added with a sneer, "with jewelry and clothing. No woman will ever trap me into marriage while there's women like that around, but they can never accuse me of being mean."

"I'm sure," laughed the other man.

Brooke had decided she had just about heard

enough of this distasteful conversation; she knocked firmly on the door and entered when bade to do so.

"Yes?" Jarrod Stone raised one dark eyebrow, his eyes broodingly gray in his deeply tanned face.

Brooke stopped in her tracks, the anger that had been the momentum behind her being able to walk into the room slowly fading. Her breath caught in her throat at the lazy smile he directed at her, leaving her momentarily speechless. When she finally did manage to speak, it was in a voice that sounded strange even to her own ears. "I, er, I ... I've brought up the model for the advertising photographs. She's waiting outside."

"Thank you." He smiled at her again, his eyes crinkling at the corners. "Would you like to show her in? My secretary's at lunch, I'm afraid."

"Certainly," she answered breathlessly.

He looked every inch the arrogant businessman sitting behind his imposing desk, and she turned in confusion to leave the room. She hesitated outside the door as she heard him give a throaty chuckle.

"You see what I mean," he said with amusement.

"What?" The other man was obviously puzzled, a younger man that she had recognized as being Philip Baylis, a business associate of the owner of Stone Computers.

"A smile and a few softly spoken words and any woman will do exactly what you ask them to, even that little mouse. She knows very well it isn't her job to bring people up to the offices, and yet she did it, anyway."

"So?"

"So that's a perfect example of what we were just discussing. No, Philip, while there are still girls like her around no woman will ever catch me in the matrimonial trap. I don't see that it's necessary when what you really want can be obtained without feeling as if you're in a cage."

Little mouse, indeed! She still felt angered at his condescension. His looks may be fantastic, but his nature wasn't so impressive, at least, not the part she had seen. But even if his words had angered her she shouldn't have played this stupid trick on him. It had been the confident way he had escorted the model out to lunch that had fired her anger anew, and given her the crazy idea of announcing her own engagement to him.

And now she had to face him. She hoped she looked more self-confident than she felt. He was likely to rip her to shreds with his tongue when he had her in his office. And it was no more than she deserved.

Today the outer office wasn't deserted. Catherine Farraday, Jarrod Stone's personal secretary, and her young assistant were both busily working as she entered the room.

Catherine gave her a cool look. "Yes?"

"Mr. Stone is expecting me. My name is Brooke Faulkner."

She gave her a disbelieving look, but buzzed through to the inner office, anyway. "A Miss Faulkner to see you, Mr. Stone."

"Send her straight in," he snapped, letting Brooke know that his temper hadn't cooled any since his telephone call down to her.

This cool beautiful girl stood up with a slight raising of her shaped, plucked eyebrows, as if she were mentally trying to work out the reason for her boss to be seeing a mere receptionist.

"I know the way," Brooke told her hurriedly, unwilling to let this girl witness her humiliation if Jarrod Stone should be unable to contain his anger and lashed out at her with his icy tongue as soon as she entered his office.

"Very well," Catherine subsided back into her chair, resuming her work with a coolly detached air.

Brooke moved through the small reception room, hesitant about actually confronting Jarrod Stone. But if she didn't go in there soon he would come out here looking for her, and she had no intention of letting him find her cowering nervously outside his office.

He bade her curtly to enter as she knocked on the door, which she reluctantly did. This time there was no charming smile for her, only a furious look on his face and an angry glitter to his eyes.

He stood up, coming around his desk to slowly walk around her as she stood in front of it. He came back to rest on the front of his desk, his arms folded in front of his powerful chest.

Even in her embarrassment Brooke could appreciate how attractive he looked, the navy blue pin-striped suit he wore fitting him as if it were tailored on him, his linen immaculate.

"So you're Brooke Faulkner," he said softly.

"Yes." Did he have to be so taunting! She was perfectly well aware that her navy pinafore dress and light blue fitted blouse in no way matched up to the expensive clothing some of the women he escorted out of the building wore. But did he have to look at her quite like that!

"The girl I'm engaged to," he continued even more softly.

She moved with a start. "I . . . I can explain about that."

He smiled, but it owed nothing to humor. "Can you now?" he mused. "You can explain how I came to be engaged to be married to a complete stranger, can you?" His light eyes snapped angrily. "It had better be a damned good explanation!"

She moved uncomfortably. "I wouldn't say that, but it is an explanation. The only trouble is I don't think you're going to like it."

He made an impatient movement to sit behind his

desk. "I don't *like* being engaged to a girl I've never met before, either!"

Brooke gasped. "Oh, that isn't true. I work here, I've seen you hundreds of times."

"Seeing isn't the same as meeting. I've seen hundreds of people many times over, but that doesn't mean I know them."

"But we have actually met," she corrected him. "I brought a model up to your office a couple of weeks ago."

He studied her for a moment. "So you did."

"And that's why I told the newspaper what I did."

"Because you brought a model up to my office?" He sounded astonished.

"Don't be ridiculous!" She had had enough of his taunts. She realized he was angry about what she had done, of course he was, but he didn't have to take this attitude with her. "I did it because I overheard your conversation that day, overheard what you had to say about women."

"Did you indeed!" His gray eyes narrowed. "And that prompted you to announce your own engagement to me? After hearing what I had to say about your own fair sex?"

"Yes, it did!" Her blue eyes deepened almost to violet. "I wanted to make you eat your words, to show you that you could be caught in the trap of matrimony as easily as any other man. But I... it didn't work out the way I intended it to. As soon as I saw it in print I knew it was wrong. But at the time I wanted only to hit out at you, to get back at you for what you think of women."

"Oh, you got back at me all right. This morning, not half an hour ago in fact, I had a telephone call from Philip Baylis congratulating me. I didn't know what the hell he was talking about," he said forcefully. "I felt like a damned fool. But I managed to bluff my way out of it. Can you imagine what it felt like to be told by a third party that I'm supposed to be getting married. I didn't even know who Brooke Faulkner was, but I did know the name sounded familiar. Then I realized that I saw it every morning when I entered the building."

"You called me a mouse that day I came up here," she reminded him resentfully.

"And for that you landed us in this mess?"

She flicked back her hair. "It will be all right. We can just announce in the next issue that it was a mistake."

He stood up again, his height making her feel very tiny, and he was so big and masculine with it—so very male. "You think it's easy as that, do you? What a ridiculous child you are. Don't you realize that by accepting Philip's congratulations this morning I as much as admitted the engagement was a real one. He has also invited the two of us to a party this evening."

"You...you didn't accept?" She frowned her nervousness.

"Of course I did. What else could I do; they all want to get a look at you. And I didn't have time to think of a good excuse not to take you along."

"You could have...could have told him we wanted to be alone this evening...to celebrate," she said desperately.

"We don't all have your devious mind."

"But you...you can't mean this engagement to stand?" Her voice was becoming shrill now.

"Oh, but I do. I'm in business. I can't be seen to become engaged one day and renounce it the next. That wouldn't do much for my reputation as a reliable businessman. Oh, no, Brooke, you started this and you can damn well see it through to the bitter end."

"The bitter end..." she echoed hollowly.

Jarrod Stone shrugged. "Just a figure of speech."

Brooke wasn't so sure—there was an inflexibility about him that pointed to him not liking to be thwarted. A pity she hadn't noticed that sooner, like two weeks ago.

"But I don't want to be engaged to you," she told him crossly.

"A pity you didn't think of that before. I'm sure you realize that I feel exactly the same way."

"Yes," she admitted guiltily, knowing that this was all her own fault.

"Mmm," he said thoughtfully. "Well, now that it seems to be public knowledge you can start acting the part. We'll meet for lunch at twelve-thirty."

"I couldn't... I couldn't go out to lunch with you. What would everyone think?" Besides, she was hardly dressed to go out with him.

"They can think what they damn well please," he muttered grimly.

"I think you've taken this far enough," she said, suddenly angry. "I admit that what I did was wrong, and I'll leave your employ straight away if that will please you." Although how she would support herself until she found another job she had no idea! "But I'm not going to let you make a fool of me—"

"I think you've managed that quite successfully without any help from me," he interrupted dryly.

"You have no right—"

"I have every right! Think of how much more of a fool you would have looked if I had denied all knowledge of you. Think of the adverse reaction you would have got from the press if I had done that. They would have hounded you to death."

She knew he was right. The trouble with her was that she hadn't thought of the consequences when she had made that stupid move, and now Jarrod Stone was going to make her pay for it. But what else had she expected—he was a well-known personality, he couldn't afford the publicity of a broken engagement. And neither could she!

She could just imagine the unpleasantness it would

cause. But she couldn't stay engaged to him, either. Just to look at him terrified the life out of her. How she had ever thought herself in love with him she would never know. She must have been mad. Yes, that must be it—at twenty years of age she was definitely past the stage of infatuation.

"Brooke?" he cut into her thoughts.

"Don't call me that!" she snapped her resentment.

"What would you have me call you—dearest, darling, my love?" he taunted.

She looked away. "Of course not!"

Jarrod Stone shrugged. "Then I'll call you Brooke. It is your name—and you are my fiancée," he added mockingly.

"I am not!"

"Oh, yes you are—until I say otherwise."

Her blue eyes widened. "And how long do you think that will be?"

"Oh, four, maybe five months," he told her carelessly.

"What!" She walked forward to rest her knuckles on the front of the desk. "Now I know you're joking."

"I rarely joke about anything this serious."

"You're...you're telling me I have to be engaged to you for *four months*?"

"At a minimum," he nodded.

"But won't that cramp your style a bit?"

"A little, but I can take it if you can. I gather there's no boyfriend...no, of course there isn't. He wouldn't exactly welcome the announcement." He straightened some papers on his desk, giving an impatient look as the telephone rang and he picked it up. "Yes, Catherine? No, and I don't want any more calls put through to me until Miss Faulkner has left." He put the receiver down, looking up at her. "Now, is there anyone I should talk to about our engagement?"

"Why on earth should you—"

"Consent, Brooke. It's usually considered polite to consult parents when contemplating marrying their daughter."

Brooke paled even more. It all sounded so...so real when he put it like that. "My parents are dead. I was brought up by a maiden aunt."

"So do I speak to her?"

"She died last year. But I hadn't had a lot to do with her for the past four years, anyway, not since she made it perfectly clear to me that she disapproved of my father marrying her sister."

"And four years ago you were...?"

"Sixteen," she admitted quietly, remembering all too well the terrible things her aunt had said to her about her father.

"That makes you twenty now. God, I'll be thought a cradle snatcher!" he muttered in disgust. "I'm thirty-seven," he added by way of explanation.

"And you've never married?" It seemed strange in this day and age to think of a man of his age not marrying.

For the first time since she had entered the room ne smiled, and she felt some of the tension start to leave her body. He sat back in the chair. "I thought about it once, when I was a couple of years older than you are at this moment. She turned me down, thank God."

"Oh."

"Right, well, I think you've taken up enough of my time for one morning. I'll see you downstairs at twelve-thirty. And arrange to have a two-hour lunch break."

"I can't do that—I have a job to do."

"And I'm your employer. Get whoever it is that usually covers for you when you're off sick to take over. And I won't expect an overshow of emotion in front of other people, but I will expect you to be a little bit more relaxed with me than you are at this moment."

"Relaxed! How can I possibly feel relaxed? I've never even spoken to you until today."

"Too bad," he said callously, standing up. "Now I'll see you out to the elevator."

Brooke stiffened. "That won't be necessary."

He opened the door for her. "But I insist. I must show a natural consideration for my brand-new fiancée," he taunted.

Her eyes were beseeching. "Please, Mr. Stone, don't—"

"Jarrod," he corrected curtly. "Call me Jarrod."

She couldn't do that! "Please don't make me go through with this. I've apologized—I don't see what else I can do to make amends."

"An apology isn't enough," he said cruelly. "I've already explained my reasons. I could make things very unpleasant for you if you prove difficult."

"I could leave." She hung back defiantly, not willing to leave his office until she had this thing settled. "You are far from being the only well-paying firm in the country."

"Oh, I know that. But with no references from here you could find things rather difficult."

"You... you can't do that! I've been a good employee."

"You call what you've just done being a good employee? Are you aware that you could land up in court for that deliberate lie you chose to tell the newspaper. I could sue you. You are quoted, so it's pretty obvious who gave them the story."

She went first pale and then red. "You... you wouldn't?"

"No, I wouldn't. But I do expect a little cooperation from you. This is your fault, after all."

"All right, all right. I'm sorry, I'm sorry, *I'm sorry!*"

Jarrod Stone looked unmoved. "Like I said, it isn't

enough." He opened the door farther. "I have an important appointment in five minutes."

"Okay, I...but what do I tell everyone?" she cried.

"Oh, tell them I've fallen madly in love with you and rushed you off your feet."

"Don't tease—*please*." Her head was bent down.

He wrenched her chin up roughly between thumb and forefinger. "I don't know what the hell else you expect me to do. I can assure you that if I did what I really want to do to you, you wouldn't like that, either."

Brooke was mesmerized by his glittering gray eyes, aware of the darkness of his skin and the tangy aftershave he wore. "What do you want to do?" she asked breathlessly.

His hand fell away and he turned her firmly out of the room. "Put you over my knee and give your backside a good thrashing. Just what you hoped to achieve, I have no idea. But still, it might prove interesting."

He silenced her as they entered his secretary's office, pausing at the door to look down at her with dark brooding eyes. Again he raised her chin, uncaring of the two curious pairs of eyes watching them. "I'll see you later, darling," he said huskily soft, but loud enough for the other two girls to hear. "We'll have lunch at the usual place."

Before Brooke could answer him his dark head swooped low and his lips fleetingly touched hers. She felt herself tremble in his arms, her eyes wide with surprise. She looked self-consciously at the girls in the room, but they were apparently busily working. She doubted they had been so engrossed a couple of seconds earlier!

Her mouth tightened. "Did you have to do that?" she muttered angrily, her almost violet eyes glaring her dislike of him.

Jarrod laughed throatily. "You say the nicest things, Brooke."

He was obviously still playing to his audience and she decided to play him at his own game, reaching up to wind her arms around his neck, her lips raised invitingly. "Just to last me until lunchtime, darling," she coaxed, reveling in the anger displayed in his deep gray eyes. "Darling?" she questioned innocently.

His grip on her arms was quite painful and it took great effort not to cry out. "Later, Brooke, later." His words sounded romantic enough, but she knew his words promised something completely different to what they were implying.

She pouted up at him. "Oh, Jarrod."

"If you don't behave yourself I'm likely to give you that good hiding I promised you," he warned her quietly.

"Oh, Jarrod, how sweet of you to say so," she smiled up at him, uncaring of the dangerous look in his eyes. "Until later, darling."

By the time she stepped out of the elevator into the reception area the two bright wings of color in her cheeks seemed be a permanent fixture. How she was going to get through the next few months, she had no idea.

Jean was looking rather harassed by this time, having difficulty managing her switchboard and also dealing with people at the desk. Brooke hadn't realized she would be so long or she wouldn't have left her alone. She had expected to be only a few minutes, just long enough to be sacked.

"What gives?" Jean asked once the rush had died down and they had a couple of minutes to themselves again. "First of all you receive a telephone call that makes you look like death and then you calmly step into the boss's private elevator and disappear for an hour."

"I'm sorry I was gone so long, Jean. I didn't mean

to leave you in the lurch like that." She shuffled the papers around on her desk, not anxious to answer the real question in Jean's words.

"So what's happened? Is someone you know ill or something?"

"Er, no." She didn't quite know how to explain what had just happened to her. She certainly couldn't tell Jean the whole truth—it would be too humiliating. "I, er, I seem to have got myself engaged."

Jean's eyes brightened with excitement. "You do? Who to?" She frowned. "You haven't mentioned seeing anyone special."

"No, well, it seems to have happened all of a sudden. I've hardly had time to think." Which was true, she certainly hadn't had time to realize exactly what this bogus engagement was going to mean to her. She did know that she had felt a strange floating sensation at the touch of Jarrod Stone's lips on her own. And also, to her shame, she had responded! Only momentarily, but it had been a definite response. But she blamed that solely on the suddenness of it, nothing else. She didn't even like the man, now, let alone imagine herself in love with him.

Jean still looked puzzled. "But what does it have to do with Jarrod Stone?"

"Everything," she said with feeling.

"Everything?" Jean's frown cleared to be replaced with a look of amazement. "But...surely you don't mean—"

"Yes, I'm engaged to Jarrod Stone."

"Goodness! But you...you can't be! I didn't even realize you were seeing him. Her face showed her disbelief.

"It has been rather sudden. I—"

"Excuse me," interrupted a husky female voice. "I'm looking for Mr. Stone's office."

Brooke turned to look at the woman, her nostrils twitching sensitively with the deep heavy perfume she wore. This woman was beautiful, absolutely beautiful. She was very tall, her blond hair shoulder length and waving provocatively around her face, her eyes a glowing green, her tiny nose uptilted and her pouting mouth painted an inviting scarlet. To Brooke she looked exquisite and she wondered who she could be—obviously one of Jarrod Stone's women, of that she felt sure. She looked the type he would go for, about thirtyish and very sophisticated.

"Mr. Stone's office is on the tenth floor," she answered politely. "If you would like to take the private elevator up I will telephone them of your arrival."

The woman nodded coolly. "Thank you, Miss... Brooke Faulkner!" Her green eyes narrowed as they looked at the gold lettering on the nameplate. " *You're* Brooke Faulkner?"

Brooke frowned. "Yes."

"Well, well, well." The woman seemed to have regained her composure. "Clever old Jarrod," she murmured to herself.

"I beg your pardon?"

The woman gave her a dazzling smile. "It isn't important. So nice to have met you, Brooke. You have helped to explain a lot."

"But I didn't do anything." She needn't have bothered to speak, the woman having already walked away from the desk to enter the elevator. How rude of her. "Who was that?" she asked Jean.

Her friend's eyes widened. "You mean you don't know?"

"I didn't get the chance to ask her," she said ruefully.

"You shouldn't have needed to. That was Selina Howard."

Brooke gasped, looking after the woman. "The wife of the multimillionaire?"

Jean nodded. "The same."

"Oh." What on earth could a woman like her want with Jarrod Stone? There seemed only one explanation and yet that didn't seem at all likely. Charles Howard was even more well-known than Jarrod Stone, and one of the richest men in the world. He was also a very good-looking man, although being in his late fifties he was much older than his thirty-year-old wife.

Brooke looked up sharply as the woman came back down again half an hour later. She must have been Jarrod Stone's important appointment, a very beautiful appointment, and it certainly wasn't a business appointment, of that she was sure. Selina Howard gave her a cool smile before leaving the building.

By the time Jarrod Stone came down in the elevator at twelve-thirty Brooke had managed to stir herself up into a very nervous state. But perhaps he just intended to have them look as if they were leaving to go to lunch together—perhaps they would part when they got outside. She hoped so.

She grabbed her leather jacket and handbag from the cloakroom before he came over, smiling nervously at the girl who was taking over for her during her lunch break. Jarrod's eyes narrowed as she reached his side, but he said nothing about her flushed cheeks and over-bright eyes, merely taking hold of her elbow to guide her out of the door opened for them by the doorman.

Once outside the building his hand dropped away and he turned left toward the shopping center, leaving Brooke to run to keep up with him, his long strides taking him along much faster than her own.

"Could you slow down a little?" she asked breathlessly.

Jarrod turned to look at her as if suddenly becoming aware of her, his pace slackening slightly, but still much too fast for her.

"Where are we going?" She looked up at him.

His mouth turned back in a sneer. "I would have thought it was obvious."

"But I...I thought we were going to lunch. It's mainly shops in this part of town."

He sighed. "One shop in particular."

"What shop is that?"

"A jeweler's. There's a very good one not far from here."

Again Brooke felt panic rising within her. "A jeweler's? Whatever for?"

"My dear girl, if we are going to be engaged you're going to need a ring. That's where we're going now—to buy you an engagement ring."

CHAPTER TWO

BROOKE STOPPED in her tracks, unconcerned when he turned to scowl his impatience. "I don't want an engagement ring," she declared.

Jarrod Stone walked back the short distance between them grasping her arm roughly and pulling her to one side of the pavement. "Don't shout like that in the street," he snapped.

She shook off his hand. "What else did you expect me to do? You were miles away from me."

"Only because you deliberately hung back, behaving hysterically. What on earth is the matter with you? Surely you realize we can't be engaged without a ring. People will be looking for that, especially this evening."

"I don't want a ring and I don't want to go out with you this evening. I don't mind keeping up this pretense at work, but I will not put on a show for all your high-class friends to laugh at."

His well-shaped mouth tightened angrily. "You say the most ridiculous things and *do* the most ridiculous things. You act far too impetuously, but I put that down to your youth. And my friends will not laugh at you, but they will think it odd if you aren't wearing my ring. This isn't something I care to discuss. I've already telephoned the jeweler's and requested he get together a selection of rings for you to look at." He looked at his wristwatch. "He's expecting us about now."

"I'm sure he'll wait for the valued customer that

you undoubtedly are. I suppose it's the place you buy all the jewelry for your women," she said bitchily, for the moment not bothered by her outspokenness. She had already far overstepped the line as far as this arrogant man was concerned and nothing she said or did now could make matters any worse for her.

"And if I do? What does that have to do with you?"

The fight went out of her at his coolness. "Nothing, I suppose."

"You suppose correctly. Now, let's go."

"Please." She held on to his arm, loving the feel of the expensive material of his suit beneath her fingers. "Don't make me do this."

His dark head was held at a haughty angle, his gray eyes unyielding. There was no doubt that he was a hard man when crossed. He must terrify his business opponents into retreat. He certainly terrified her. "Must I keep reminding you that you started this?"

"But do you have to take advantage of it?" Her eyes pleaded with him.

"Yes. Now that's the last time we discuss this. From now on you'll just do as you're told. And there will be no repeat of your behavior this morning," he added warningly.

They were walking along side by side, now, he at last seeming to realize that she had shorter legs than he did. She looked up at him innocently.

"Did I do something wrong?" she asked, knowing very well to what he referred.

"The way you drooled over me was completely unnecessary. I told you I wanted no overshow of emotion."

"Oh, I didn't *drool*!"

"You gave a very good impression of it." His eyes remained fixed ahead.

"You kissed me first," she accused.

"I admit that, but it was nothing like the provocative act you were putting on." He stopped outside an expensive looking jeweler's. "I don't want anything like that in here, just a little natural affection for a new fiancé."

"I hate you, Jarrod Stone!"

He looked down at her with enigmatic eyes, making her aware of just how attractive he was—so tall and commanding; really majestically male; and very, very handsome. She felt the old familiar flutterings in her stomach. It seemed she wasn't over her infatuation after all!

"Let's just keep it that way, shall we," he said softly. "I must admit to feeling slightly curious about your motivation for announcing our engagement this morning. At first I imagined it to be a not very subtle form of blackmail, then after reading your file, your age and so forth, I wondered if it might not be infatuation."

"Not for this girl," she answered quickly. It *had* been infatuation, but that infatuation had quickly turned to dislike. His contemptuous words had turned her supposed love into a desire for revenge on his mercenary attitude toward women. He was the sort of man women fell for in the hundreds, and he walked away from them all untouched. Well, she had just made sure he hadn't got away so easily this time.

"Why so vehement? It wouldn't be the first time a young girl has imagined herself in love with an older man. Some of these girls have been known to take the initiative when they don't think they are achieving their aim fast enough."

"Like I said, not this girl."

"No, your move was made from pure revenge, wasn't it, little mouse?"

She knew he was deliberately baiting her and she obstinately refused to let him ruffle her. "Can we get this over with? I have to be back in forty minutes."

His eyes snapped with anger. "I thought I told you to get an extended lunch break."

Brooke pretended an interest in the jewelry window. "You did," she confirmed disinterestedly.

"Then why the hell didn't you?"

She flung back her head, her hair gleaming auburn brown in the sunlight. "I didn't because I'm not the owner of the firm. I can't just take two-hour lunch breaks when I feel in the mood."

"You're engaged to the owner—that amounts to the same thing."

"I would have thought that was all the more reason for me not to take advantage of the situation. By the way, there's a little man bobbing around inside the jeweler's. I think he's looking at us."

"No doubt. Well, if you only have forty minutes left I suppose we had better get inside."

The jeweler had obviously seen Jarrod Stone numerous times before and she wondered if she had been right in her assumption about this place. That he was a valued customer there could be no doubt, it was there in the overshow of respect he was receiving.

"So nice to see you again," the jeweler gushed. "And to meet your fiancée." He smiled at Brooke. "I'm so glad you chose our establishment to buy your ring, Miss Faulkner."

Jarrod gave what Brooke considered to be his first natural smile of the day, at least, in her company. "You know you're the best in town, Green."

"So kind of you to say so. And may I say I agree with your decision not to include sapphires in your choice. Miss Faulkner's eyes *are* more violet than blue."

"Could we see the rings?" Jarrod requested tersely. "We don't have a lot of time." This last comment was obviously meant for Brooke.

She waited until the jeweler had left them alone before making a comment. "I didn't realize you had even noticed the color of my eyes."

"I didn't," he replied curtly. "It was in your file."

"Didn't your secretary think it odd for you to want to read my file?"

"I don't pay her to think about my personal life."

Brooke frowned. "I'm sure it didn't say anywhere in my file that my eyes were violet."

"Maybe not. But they are, so let's not argue about it." He straightened as the tray of rings was presented for their inspection.

They were beautiful rings, diamond clusters, solitaires, emeralds and rubies surrounded by sparkling diamonds—and all of them looking as if they would cost a fortune! She felt sure they all would. This was one of those exclusive, expensive jeweler's that only the very rich frequented. And Jarrod Stone was very rich.

Her eyes glowed as she picked up first one ring and then another, almost afraid to touch them, but tempted by their beauty. As she had very long slender hands some of the smaller stones just didn't look right on her finger, but she chose these rings to try on because she knew they would be the least expensive. Finally she looked up at Jarrod for help. "Which one do you like?" she asked helplessly.

Without hesitation he chose a large diamond set on a thin gold band, sliding it onto her finger before she had time to protest. "That's the one," he nodded his approval.

She could tell by the satisfied smile on the jeweler's face that Jarrod had chosen the most expensive ring on the tray. She tried to pull it off her finger, but Jarrod's strong brown hand came out to stop her movements.

"You may as well leave it on," he told her. "It fits perfectly."

"Oh, but I—"

Mr. Green had already picked up the tray containing the other rings and was in the process of locking them away again.

"No arguments in here, please, Brooke," Jarrod warned her out of earshot of the other man.

"But this ring is much too expensive," she protested.

"Leave that to me. That's the ring I want you to wear."

"But I'll be frightened of losing it." She looked down at it wide-eyed.

"It will be insured," he said uncaringly.

"Yes, but—"

"Leave it, Brooke," he ordered as Mr. Green came back.

Brooke felt a curiosity to know just how much this rock on her finger was going to cost, but she knew it wasn't expected of her to stay and listen to the money side of the sale and so she wandered over to look in some of the other cabinets, looking at the glittering necklaces inside.

Once outside Jarrod handed her a large square box, ignoring her questioning look. "Open it," he ordered.

She did so with trembling fingers, crying out her surprise as she saw the contents. Nestling in blue velvet was a large teardrop diamond set on the most delicately fine gold chain she had ever seen, and lying within its circle were a pair of matching earrings. They were really lovely.

She thrust them back at him. "I don't want these." She remembered too well what he had said about giving his women jewelry. "The ring I'll wear until I can be free of you, but I don't have to accept anything else from you."

"They're for you to wear tonight." He ignored the proffered box. "I want you to look the part."

"And a little receptionist like myself isn't likely to have this sort of jewelry hidden away," she sneered.

"Exactly," he agreed cruelly.

"You're an arrogant swine, Jarrod Stone. But I'll

wear your diamonds for you—as long as I can return them to you as soon as we've left the party."

"Don't be so childish."

"Then I won't wear them. You can't force me to," she declared obstinately.

"What an obstructive little girl you are. All right, I'll keep them locked up for you. Now let's go on to a shop where we can buy you a gown."

Brooke stiffened. "I have my own clothes, thank you."

"I'm sure you have, but I want you to have something new."

"I have my own clothes," she repeated through gritted teeth. As it happened she had exactly the right gown to wear to go out with this sophisticated man, a gown that had been bought for a special occasion that had never taken place. It was an expensive gown, bought to impress a boyfriend that she had finished with before the promised evening out. At the time he simply hadn't measured up to her rather romantic impression of Jarrod Stone. How ironic that she should now wear the gown to go out with Jarrod Stone himself.

"Do you have to argue about everything?" he snapped.

"If it means I hold on to my identity against you— yes!" she answered defiantly.

"God, you're impossible!" He hailed a passing taxi, bundling her inside before sitting beside her. "Before you start a full-scale argument in the street," he explained.

"You're too dominant, that's your trouble."

He began to smile and finally the smile turned into a genuine laugh. It changed his whole face, not making him appear quite so grim and also making him look younger. Brooke felt her senses stir at the real humor in his deep gray eyes.

"*I'm* dominant?" he chuckled. "You seem to be the one organizing my life for me at the moment."

He got out and opened the door for her as they reached the building he owned. "I'll pick you up at eight-thirty this evening."

"But you don't know where I...oh, yes, my file."

"Mmm, it has your address in it. Not much else, but it does have that. I'll see you later." He got back into the taxi.

Too late Brooke realized she still had the necklace and earrings in her hand. She would have to keep them with her now, something she hadn't wanted to do. Her handbag seemed the best place to stow them away, and putting the case at the bottom of what she jokingly called her "shoulder suitcase" she went back to her desk.

She was so conscious of the huge diamond on her finger that for the first half an hour after her return she kept her left hand hidden. Jean soon noticed it though, exclaiming enthusiastically over its beauty.

"You still haven't told me how you came to be in love and engaged to him. Why only this morning I was insulting him to you, doubting his ability to be passionate if he tried. Now you must know firsthand that I was wrong."

She didn't know firsthand at all, but his full, sensuous lower lip didn't point to him being the cold impassionate machine Jean had implied this morning. And he hadn't kissed like an amateur, that brief caress evoking a response within her in spite of herself.

"You were wrong," she confirmed, sure that this was so.

Jean smiled dreamily. "It's all like a fairy tale, isn't it? Engaged to be married to the unattainable Jarrod Stone. Lucky old you."

YES, LUCKY old her. She wasn't thinking that way later that evening as she nervously got herself ready to go to Philip Baylis's party. If Selina Howard was an example of Jarrod Stone's friends, then there would be some really sophisticated people at this party tonight.

Her gown was a russet-colored silk, bringing out the red lights in her dark brown hair. It clung in soft folds over her breasts and hips, the high rolled neckline adding to the fragility of her swanlike neck, the long sleeves finishing in a point at the wrist. It was a gown that emphasized her slenderness and suited her like no other gown she had ever possessed.

She had washed her hair and brushed it dry until it gleamed reddish brown, crackling with health and cleanliness. She had applied a light eye makeup and mascara, brushing a soft peach lip gloss over her lips. The earrings and necklace glittered in glowing beauty against the dark material of her gown and she knew she was looking her best.

Jarrod Stone's dark gray eyes gleamed his approval of her as she let him into her tiny apartment. He was looking particularly attractive tonight, wearing black trousers, a white silk shirt, and a gray velvet jacket that matched the steely gray of his eyes. He carried a large white box under one arm and Brooke had to admit to feeling curious about its contents.

He stood back to survey her. "Very nice," he said finally, placing that intriguing box on the table.

Brooke blushed prettily. "Thank you. Tonight, you...you won't leave me on my own too much? I...I don't know any of the people who are likely to be at this party."

"You'll know Philip."

She gave a throaty chuckle. "I don't *know* Philip Baylis—I've only seen him a couple of times when he's come to see you. I know about him, as I know about you, but I don't actually know him."

"You soon will," he said dryly. "I have no doubt that Philip will waste little time introducing himself to you. But don't ever forget that you're supposed to be engaged to me," he added warningly.

"I can hardly forget it with this huge rock weighing my finger down," she retorted hotly, resenting his implication that she was stupid enough to flirt with his friends. "You didn't even bother to ask me if I wanted this ring. I may not have liked it," she said petulantly.

Jarrod shrugged. "It isn't important."

"Only that it looks expensive enough to be worn by the fiancée of the great Jarrod Stone," she scorned. "You're enjoying this, Mr. Stone, enjoying the fact that I stupidly got myself engaged to you."

"I'm not enjoying it at all, Brooke," he contradicted grimly. "But I have little choice about it, so I mean to make the best of it. You would do well to do the same. After all, isn't that partly the reason you did it. You denied infatuation, so it must have been partly blackmail."

"It was pure revenge," she denied hotly.

"If you like to think so. Nevertheless, the jewelry you now have in your possession will bring you a sizable sum when you decide to sell it. That should make it all the easier for you to bear being engaged to a man you say you hate. For some reason women seem to find jewelry a great comfort."

"This jewelry isn't mine to sell," Brooke told him fiercely. "The earrings and necklace I'll return at the end of the evening, the ring when you decide you've punished me enough for my impetuosity. Whether you believe me or not, blackmail didn't enter into my thoughts at all. I once believed myself—"

"Yes?" he prompted at her hesitation.

She shook her head. Why should she give him the satisfaction of knowing she had once thought herself in love with him. He would probably laugh in her face at such an admission. "It isn't important. Shouldn't we be leaving now? It's getting late."

"I suppose so." He picked up the box he had carried in, handing it to her. "I realize this should be

mink or ermine, but I don't happen to believe in
killing animals to provide a woman with something
beautiful to wear."

She gave him a puzzled look, ripping off the lid to
the box to stare at its contents. Lying among the tissue paper was a snowy white velvet cape. She picked it
up, smoothing its softness lovingly. "It's beautiful,"
she said breathlessly.

"Good." He took it out of her hand, draping it
casually around her shoulders. "We'd better be going
now."

His car was fast and sleek, moving with a speed that
was completely effortless. It was a dark green Ferrari,
and the man at her side drove it with a skill that was
purely habitual. It seemed incredible to Brooke that
she was actually sitting here at his side on her way out
with him for the evening.

Philip Baylis's house was about ten miles out of the
center of London, a house set back off the road and
reached by a long gravel driveway leading right up to
the oak front door. Cars adorned the driveway and the
whole house was bathed in light. Soft music sounded
from inside and Brooke followed Jarrod Stone up to
the front door with some trepidation.

They were admitted by a manservant, Brooke leaving her cape in his capable hands. Jarrod turned to
look at her. "I suppose you want to powder your nose
or whatever it is that women do when they disappear
for hours on end?"

"Yes, please." Her hair could definitely do with a
tidy up.

"It's through there," he pointed to a door on the
left. "I'll be inside having a drink."

"Oh, but—"

"Don't be such a baby," he said impatiently. "I
won't be far away."

She set her mouth determinedly and entered the
powder room. There were several other women in

here and she moved through them awkwardly to the large mirror along one wall, brushing her hair self-consciously.

"I notice Jarrod hasn't arrived, yet," remarked a tall blond girl to another girl standing a few feet away.

"He'll be here. Philip said he invited him," the brunette replied.

"I can hardly wait." The blonde applied her lipstick.

Brooke had remained rooted to the spot at the first mention of Jarrod's name, curious to find out what was going to be said next. Both these girls were beautiful, perhaps they had been some of the girls Jarrod was reputed to have escorted over the last few years.

"Have you seen this girl?" the brunette asked.

"Never. No one seems to have heard of her until today. He really kept quiet about this one."

"Selina won't be very happy about it," the brunette laughed bitchily. "She really thought she had him where she wanted him."

The blonde arched one thinly plucked eyebrow. "I'm sure she's had him *there*, several times."

"You think it actually went that far?"

"Charles is such a simpleton where Selina is concerned. He has no control over her at all. And she wanted Jarrod, we all know that."

The brunette nodded slowly. "But I wouldn't have thought Jarrod—"

"He's a man, Sonia, and Selina *is* very beautiful." She frowned. "This engagement of Jarrod's is all a bit sudden, a bit too convenient if you ask me."

The girl called Sonia looked puzzled. "What do you mean?"

"Well, it could all be a ruse, couldn't it? Jarrod could have persuaded some poor creature into believing that she is in love with him and that he feels the same way about her. Charles would never suspect anything between Selina and Jarrod with him a newly engaged man."

"I suppose so. There was quite a lot of gossip going around. I'm sure Charles must have heard some of it."

"You see what I mean. I bet this girl of Jarrod's is a real little mouse."

The use of that name for her was enough to snap Brooke out of her stunned silence, but before she could actually say anything someone else came into the room and the other two girls wandered back outside to the party, still gossiping.

So that was Jarrod's little game! Furious color flooded her cheeks. Jarrod Stone was using her to cover up his own affair with a married woman. How dare he! Of all the despicable things to do. All the time he had been making out he was the wronged person in all this, when really it suited him to be an engaged man right now.

No wonder Selina Howard had rushed over to see him this morning. But she had soon been reassured when she had seen Brooke, knowing she had absolutely no competition in her. And Jarrod must have reassured her even more when she was up in his office with him.

How dare he! How dare he use her in this way. He was disgusting, covering up his own behavior by taking advantage of this situation. He was having an affair with Selina Howard and using her to shield it from the woman's husband.

But what could she do about it? There was no way she could get herself out of this engagement, not without causing embarrassment to both of them. Besides, Jarrod had made it perfectly clear he had no intention of releasing her. His obstinacy now became transparently clear.

But she wouldn't let him think he had got away with fooling her. Oh, no, she would make sure she let him know about his sordid little affair being known to her. And she wouldn't feel guilty any more. Why should she?

It didn't take her long to find Jarrod among the crowd, his height and distinguished appearance making him conspicuous. She moved swiftly through the people to be at his side.

Jarrod turned to look down at her flushed face and gleaming eyes, raising one eyebrow questioningly. "I thought you'd got lost."

She took the glass of bubbly liquid he held out to her, flicking back her head haughtily, ignoring the curious stares of the other people. "You don't seem to be particularly bothered even if I had," she replied coolly, sipping the chilled champagne.

He frowned. "What's the matter with you?"

Brooke looked up at him challengingly. "Why should there be anything wrong with me? I've merely been tidying my hair."

"For fifteen minutes?"

She shrugged. "I have a lot of hair."

"Now look, Brooke—"

His angry words were cut off by the appearance of their host at his side. "She's turned up then, Jarrod," Philip Baylis grinned good-naturedly, putting his hand out to Brooke politely. "I'm very pleased to meet you."

She smiled shyly, meeting his gesture. "Thank you."

He looked at the grim face of his friend. "She's lovely, Jarrod. You'll have to keep your eye on her among this pack of wolves." He smiled at Brooke again. "You should be safe with Jarrod by your side."

"That's providing he remains there." She gave her fiancé a sly look.

Jarrod's fingers dug painfully into her soft flesh as he put his arm around her shoulders. "Where else would I go?" he teased, but his eyes told a different story, warning her to behave.

"I have no idea," she returned softly.

"This isn't a line," laughed Philip, seemingly unaware of the tension between them. "But haven't I seen you somewhere before?"

"Possibly. I work for Jarrod." That grip on her shoulders tightened even more and she winced with the pain of it.

Philip looked astounded. "You do?"

"Mmm," she nodded, taking no notice of the looks she was receiving from Jarrod. "I'm the receptionist."

"So you are." His amazement was obvious. "You sly devil, Jarrod," he slapped the other man on the shoulder. "Keeping her hidden away like that."

"Jarrod likes to keep secrets," Brooke put in softly.

He gave her a sharp look. "Not from you, darling," he drawled.

She gave him a cold angry look. "Even from me."

Philip laughed. "I'm sure he doesn't. He's a reformed person, engaged to be married and all that. It was the shock of my life this morning when I saw your engagement announced in the newspaper."

"No more of a shock than it was to Jarrod," she smiled tightly.

"Mmm, he seemed rather bowled over when I spoke to him this morning."

"No doubt he was," she agreed.

"Only because it wasn't supposed to be announced just yet," Jarrod put in calmly. "But you know how the press gets hold of these things."

Philip grimaced. "Oh, I know the press all right." His attention was caught and held by a woman on the other side of the room and he excused himself before going over to her.

Brooke sipped her champagne, pointedly ignoring the man at her side as she looked around her disinterestedly.

"What the hell is the matter with you?" Jarrod demanded tautly.

She gave him a chilling look. "I'm perfectly all right, thank you."

"I wasn't asking you if you were all right, I asked you what was the matter with you! You're...you're different, more—"

"More self-confident you mean. But then why shouldn't I be? You're not such a great person after all, are you? I think you're disgusting!" she spat the words at him, glaring her dislike. "And I actually felt guilty about playing this trick on you. You deserve all that you get—and more!"

Jarrod's mouth tightened and he retained his temper with effort. "What the hell are you talking about?"

"You know very well what I'm talking about so don't try to act the innocent with me. I never would have believed you could stoop so low. To—"

"Jarrod!"

Brooke didn't need to turn to know who that voice belonged to—Selina Howard! And she was smiling in an intimate way at Jarrod, her arm through his. But of course, they didn't need to worry about gossip now, not now that Jarrod was engaged to her! Oh, it was so humiliating to be used in this way.

She watched the two of them, watched the way Selina Howard made Jarrod bend his head so that she could whisper in his ear, the way he laughed throatily at whatever it was she had said to him.

It was several minutes before either of them seemed to become aware of her still standing there. Finally it was Selina Howard who turned to include her in the conversation.

"We meet again, Brooke," she said softly, her green eyes assessing as they took in Brooke's figure-hugging gown. "I'm sure you didn't expect it to be so soon."

"I didn't expect it at all, Mrs. Howard," she replied shortly.

The tall beautiful woman gave a tinkling laugh, but the humor didn't reach her hard, pebble-green eyes. "Please call me Selina," she invited graciously. "Being Jarrod's fiancée you're sure to see a lot of me in future."

Brooke raised an eyebrow. "Really?"

"Oh, yes. Jarrod and I are great friends," Selina Howard informed her triumphantly.

"And your husband." She smiled sweetly at them. "We mustn't forget your husband. Where is he, by the way?"

"Charles is in Europe at the moment."

"How convenient for you."

"I beg your pardon?" Those green eyes narrowed dangerously.

"I said how miserable for you," Brooke replied.

"Yes, isn't it." She glowed up at Jarrod. "But friends always help to ease the loneliness. Jarrod has been so good to me during Charles's absence."

"I'm sure he has. But he could be rather preoccupied in future, arranging the wedding and things like that," she smiled glowingly at Jarrod, uncaring of the scowl on his face. "There's always such a lot to organize. You must realize that, being married yourself."

A faint flush colored the other woman's pale cheeks. "When is the wedding to be?"

"We—"

"Oh, quite soon," Brooke interrupted him. "We have no reason to wait. Jarrod's very anxious that the wedding should take place soon, aren't you, darling?"

He looked thunderous, and she knew that once they were alone he would let her feel the full force of his anger. But she didn't care about that now. He wasn't going to get away with making a fool out of her.

Selina Howard looked less sure of herself now, looking uncertainly from Jarrod to Brooke. "I didn't realize you had already set a date. You've only just become engaged."

Brooke looked deliberately shy. "The engagement is only a formality as far as Jarrod and I are concerned. The marriage will take place next month."

Jarrod looked visibly startled, his expression becoming grimmer as she calmly met his furious gaze. "I thought we had agreed not to disclose that," he said tautly.

She smiled at him. "As Mrs. Howard is such a good friend of yours, it can't possibly matter if we tell her. Besides, we'll be sending out the invitations quite soon. We wouldn't want Mrs. Howard to be too shocked when she receives hers, now would we?"

Selina Howard's head flicked back haughtily. "I'll call you tomorrow, Jarrod. Goodbye, Brooke."

"Oh, surely not goodbye," she returned sweetly. "As you said, we'll be seeing a lot of each other."

Another cool look was directed at her before Selina Howard swept away from them, leaving behind a cloud of perfume. That perfume seemed to belong exclusively to her, and Brooke wouldn't be at all surprised if that wasn't the case. Charles Howard was rich enough to buy a hundred perfumes exclusively for the use of his wife if he wanted to.

Brooke looked innocently up at Jarrod, sipping her champagne with cool deliberation. "She's very beautiful."

Jarrod grasped her arm, his fingers pressing painfully into her flesh. "Selina Howard's looks don't seem important right at this moment," he muttered between gritted teeth.

"Really? They seemed very important to you this morning."

He frowned darkly. "This morning?"

"Your important appointment."

"Oh...oh, yes. Forget that for a moment," he said, dismissing her remark. "Why did you tell her we were getting married next month? What game are you playing, now."

"No game, Mr. Stone. I just don't like being used."

He shook his head dazedly. "*You're* being used? I thought that was my fate?"

"So did I. I even felt sorry for you, but not any-more. You disgust me."

"That's the second time you've said that. You were like this when you came back from the powder room. What happened in there?"

"How clever of you to guess," she smiled at him brightly. "Just a couple of your so-called friends hav-ing a cosy little chat about you. Quite enlightening really."

"Let's leave," Jarrod said abruptly. "We can talk about this better alone. Wait here while I make our excuses."

"I would prefer to wait outside."

"I said wait here."

"I'll be outside," she declared stubbornly, moving away before he could stop her. She could imagine what construction his friends would put on their early departure. Let them think what they liked! She didn't care as long as she knew in her own mind that it wasn't true.

At least she had got back at him for using her, stir-ring things up a little between him and his mistress. Not that she thought he would have much difficulty explaining his way out of that, but no doubt Selina Howard would give him a difficult time for a while. Good, she thought spitefully.

"Why are you always so damned stubborn?" Jar-rod demanded on the way home.

"I'm not stubborn. I just don't like to be bullied."

"What did these so-called friends of mine have to say? I take it that is the reason for your attitude?"

"Oh, they just told me of your sordid little affair with Mrs. Howard. Well, I wouldn't exactly say they *told* me. They were discussing it between them, I just happened to be there at the time." She made a deter-mined effort not to look at him.

"My *affair* with Selina?" he repeated softly.

"Yes."

"And that's why you told her we were getting married next month?"

"Yes. She looked quite worried when I told her that," she said with satisfaction.

"So did I," he admitted grimly. "I've never met anyone as impetuous as you are. I'm only surprised you haven't got yourself into more trouble than you have. Do you realize that by the end of this evening the fact that our wedding is to be next month will be all over London?"

Now she did look at him, her mouth dropping open. "Surely Mrs. Howard wouldn't—"

"No, she wouldn't. But you said it loud enough for several other people to hear. Believe me, by tomorrow everyone will be expecting their invitation to our wedding!"

CHAPTER THREE

Her hand flew up to her pale cheek. "Oh, no!"

"Oh, yes," he said curtly.

"Surely they wouldn't—"

"I tell you they will."

"Oh, God!" Now what had she done! Things seemed to go from bad to worse as far as she and Jarrod Stone were concerned. And it was all her own doing!

Jarrod sighed. "I thought an engagement was bad enough, but this is something else completely. Marriages aren't so easy to get out of."

"I'm not marrying you!"

"You may damn well have to," he told her shortly.

She wrenched the ring from her finger, throwing it onto the dashboard of the car. "I won't do anything I don't want to! You were using me to cover up your affair with Selina Howard, but I won't be a party to that anymore. No doubt she'll soon get over her anger with you at my saying we were getting married and you can carry on as you have been doing."

"So you've already decided that what you heard was the truth?"

"Oh, yes. She was your important appointment, remember? I suppose you told her then of our phony engagement. It really gave her a shock when I said we were getting married. so you can keep your ring and explain to your mistress that it was all a mistake, that I was just being bitchy."

Jarrod sat forward and picked up the ring, watching as it glittered and shone. He thrust it at her. "Put it back on. The engagement still stands. Nothing has changed since this morning."

"It has as far as I'm concerned," she said shrilly. "I've found out about your mistress and I won't help you to fool Charles Howard."

"You will do as you're told. My threat about your future employment still stands. Put the ring on," he ordered.

"I don't want to. You still haven't asked me if I like it," she added resentfully, pushing it back on her finger when he seemed adamant that she should.

"Do you?"

"Well, yes, but I— That isn't the point! You didn't bother to ask me earlier."

"I've asked you now. Be satisfied with that."

"Mr. Stone, I—"

"For God's sake call me Jarrod!"

"Do you have to be so angry all the time?" Brooke quavered. "It isn't easy to suddenly be thrust into this intimacy with you when for the last six months I've thought of you as nothing but my boss. It doesn't seem right for me to be calling you Jarrod."

"Do you know, Brooke, until this morning I believed myself to be quite a patient man. Since meeting you all that's changed. Everything about you angers me—your stubbornness, your impetuosity, just about everything. But until a few minutes ago I thought I was handling this situation with moderate calm." He ignored her snort of disbelief. "That was until your tongue ran away with you just once too often, as it did just now. I hope you will have more forbearance over the weekend."

Brooke's eyes widened. "Over the weekend?"

"Mmm, something else I'm sure you hadn't thought of." He gave a wry smile. "My mother and father have invited us down to their country estate for the weekend."

Her heart sank. "I didn't know you had any family."

"Oh, yes, besides my mother and father I have a brother of twenty-two and a sister of eighteen. I need hardly say that they are all anxious to meet you."

His taunting voice angered her. "Did you have to tell them? Surely we didn't have to involve your family in all this?"

Jarrod stopped the car outside the building that contained her apartment, turning to face her in the confines of the car. "I didn't tell them—you did."

"I didn't—"

"They found out the same way I did, Brooke. The only difference being that they were pleased about it."

She suddenly felt breathless by his closeness. He may be arrogant and cynical but he was still the most handsome man she had ever seen. Tonight at the party he had easily stood out as the most attractive man there, a certain aloofness about him making him a challenge to any woman.

Brooke felt her old stirrings of attraction toward him—the longings she had had to be in his arms and be loved by him. But he had never even noticed her until this morning when he could do little else, and she hadn't been brought to his attention in a way that would endear her to him.

But then he was never likely to be attracted to her, anyway, not with someone as beautiful as Selina Howard in his life. No, she knew her own limitations, she may be moderately attractive but she could never be called beautiful. She would have to leave Jarrod Stone to women like the lovely Selina Howard, women who understood the sophisticated games he engaged in.

But that didn't stop her feeling attracted to him now, didn't stop her being completely aware of him. She should have remained adamant when she had handed him back his ring and not been browbeaten into putting it back on. But she wouldn't marry him, no matter how she had committed herself in the hearing of all those people. She wouldn't be strong enough to hold out against him and she had no intention of being his wife while he had the other woman as his mistress.

She looked away from the warmth in his gray eyes. "Your family want you to get married?"

"My brother and sister consider me quite ancient not to have settled down, as they put it, with a family of my own. I'm sure you think the same way, you're about their age," he said almost thoughtfully.

"You could hardly marry when the woman in your life is already married," she put in bitchily, still reeling under his potent attraction—and resenting every moment of it.

"That's true," he agreed mildly. "I think my family are going to like you. You have my mother's way of thinking, black is black and white is white and gray is just a lighter shade of black."

"I wouldn't consider you gray, Mr. Stone. You're definitely black."

"As the devil, hmm?" he mocked.

"Himself," she nodded agreement.

"My mother is going to love you," he smiled. "She considers my behavior reprehensible."

"I think I'm going to like your mother, too."

Jarrod watched her closely, that smile still on his lips. "You're not at all as I imagined you to be."

"As you . . . as you *imagined* me to be?" she sounded her surprise. "I didn't think you even knew I existed." This conversation was proving interesting.

"Oh, yes." He settled back more comfortably in his seat, stretching his long legs out before him. "Can you see me missing a beautiful woman?" he taunted. "You always looked a cool little thing, sitting there behind that huge desk, always neat, always tidy."

"I'm not little," she said crossly. "You keep calling me that."

"You seem little to me, you must be at least a foot shorter than me."

"I should think so, you're at least six foot two."

"Six four, actually."

"Well, then, at five feet two I consider myself medium height for a woman."

"You see what I mean, your appearance is deceptive. You're a fiery little thing, quite surprising really."

"I have a temper like anyone else, but I'm not fiery," she denied.

"Oh, yes, you are. I never would have thought it with those pansy-blue eyes of yours." He sat up suddenly, his look cool again. "Isn't it time you disappeared like Cinderella?"

Brooke stiffened. "I don't consider myself to be in the least like Cinderella. But I mustn't keep you from your...your friends. It's only eleven-thirty, I'm sure you have no intention of going to bed yet, at least, not your own."

"You see, another surprise," he didn't appear to be angered by her words—more amused. "I wouldn't have thought the sweet little thing I considered you to be capable of such terrible thoughts. Charles Howard may be away from home but I have no intention of sharing his wife's bed in his absence."

Brooke turned to open the car door. "Then maybe it will be your own bed you occupy, but not alone."

"I never sleep alone," he told her softly. "I have a rather large cat called Rupert who insists on sleeping at the foot of my bed." He laughed openly at her indignation. "You shouldn't jump to conclusions, little girl."

"Will you stop calling me that!"

Jarrod shook his head slowly. "I think perhaps I should keep reminding myself that's what you are. You can be quite attractive when you're angry. But I don't play with little girls," he added harshly.

She thrust the door open far enough for her to get out. "Good night, Mr. Stone!"

"Brooke!" he stopped her just as she was about to slam the door shut behind her.

"Yes?" she asked tautly, deliberately averting her head.

"I'll pick you up at two-thirty tomorrow, that way we'll arrive in time for tea," he informed her.

"How nice," she retorted sarcastically. "Are you sure that when it comes to dinner I'll know which knives and forks to use."

With a slam of his own car door he came quickly around to her side, wrenching her startled face around to meet his look. "You can dislike me all you want, Brooke, but leave my family out of this vendetta you have against me. I won't have you being sarcastic about any member of my family. Don't you think it's time you snapped out of this persecution complex of yours and stopped thinking everyone is putting you down all the time?"

"Why you—" Her hand flew up but it never made contact with his arrogant face, his fingers passing around her wrist and squeezing so tightly she felt sure he had cut off her circulation. "You bast—"

"Don't say it, Brooke," he threatened. "That's the foulest word in the English language."

Her eyes were purple with feeling. "Then it suits you perfectly."

"You little hellcat!" he said fiercely. "If you have to hate me I might as well give you a damn good reason for it!"

He pulled her roughly against him, bending his head to loom over her for several long seconds. Brooke watched him as if in a dream, watching as he slowly lowered his head, his lips claiming hers in a kiss that was totally savage. He forced her lips apart, his arms like steel bands as she struggled to be free.

He persisted in that kiss until all the fight went out of her, her whole body feeling bruised. Against her will she found herself responding, her mouth moving beneath his as the kiss became gentler, Jarrod's mouth caressing now rather than demanding.

Brooke's arms moved up around his neck, his hands moving searchingly across her back. This was incredible! Jarrod Stone was kissing her, and she liked it, loved it even. His mouth and body had taken possession of her in a way that was totally masterful.

He put her away from him as quickly as he had pulled her into his arms. "Get inside!" he ordered harshly. "I'll see you tomorrow."

She made her way slowly up to her apartment, still dazed from his unexpected kiss. That he was a master of the art she had no doubt, her burning anger soon turning to something completely different. Instead of making her hate him he had just confirmed that she was in love with him!

BROOKE HAD BEEN very nervous about meeting Jarrod again, but she needn't have bothered, he was acting as if nothing had happened between them. If anything he was acting cooler than ever toward her, not having spoken more than a few sentences to her since she had got in the car.

He was looking vitally attractive in cream trousers and a black fitted shirt, turned back at the cuffs to expose a tanned length of arm, the hair here lighter than the raven sheen of his head. His clothing was more casual than anything else she had ever seen him wear and it made her all the more aware of him.

Not that she needed to be made any more aware of him, her senses already heightened to the rip-cord muscle beneath his shirt, the strong column of his throat and that strong handsome face that made her heart flutter just to look at him.

But his eyes could be so chillingly cutting, so disdainful, and she hadn't forgotten what his own temper could lead them to. Not that she had minded that part of his anger.

"What are you thinking about?" he asked abruptly.

"I was just thinking about your family," she lied.
"Do your brother and sister work?"

He gave her a hard look as if doubting these had been her thoughts at all. "My sister is at college... art," he added in disgust. "Dave's at medical school."

"What's your sister's name?" Anything was better than their former silence.

"Angie," he supplied shortly.

"And is Angie good at art?" she continued, trying to draw him out.

He gave a slight smile. "She says she is."

"And is she?"

"Not bad, I suppose. Don't worry, you'll have plenty of opportunity to judge for yourself. I have no doubt she'll show you around her studio. Dave will probably want to know your medical history. Don't tell him," he warned. "By the time he's finished with you, you'll wonder how many days you have left. Angie and Dave are an incorrigible pair. But you'li soon find that out for yourself."

"They sound... frightening." And they did to someone who had been an only child brought up by a maiden aunt. She had always been a little shy with people her own age, never having mixed with a lot of other children out of school hours.

Jarrod gave a throaty chuckle. "That's the one thing they aren't. A highly spirited pair, perhaps, but not frightening."

"What have you done with your cat this weekend?"

"I have a housekeeper."

"Oh, of course," she blushed. "I should have guessed."

"I'm a lousy cook," he offered by way of explanation. "Eggs and bacon are about my limit. Besides, it beats having a wife."

"One of your own, anyway," she put in softly.

His mouth tightened. "I don't want any of those comments in front of my parents," he told her angrily. "They wouldn't understand your reason for doing it."

"As long as you do."

"I know why you *think* you're doing it. But none of this in front of my family, agreed?" he quirked an eyebrow at her.

"I suppose so. I don't want to make the weekend any more difficult by having your family dislike me. That I can do without."

"Mmm, it could prove difficult if we let it. A little bit of acting on your part and it could all pass off quite smoothly. I told them we would stay until after lunch tomorrow."

Brooke felt a sense of apprehension. "When you say acting, you mean..?"

His look was cruel. "I mean a little of that show you put on for my secretary yesterday morning. My family would appreciate it more than she did," he said dryly.

She shook her head. "I couldn't, I couldn't do that. Yesterday I did it because... well, because—"

"Because you wanted to get back at me," Jarrod finished for her.

"Yes," she agreed unhesitantly.

He swung the car down a long gravel driveway. A huge red-brick building stood in the midst of sweeping green lawns and neat flower beds. The front door of the house stood open in the heat of the day, and a young girl ran out to greet them as Jarrod parked the car in the driveway.

"Jarrod!" she squealed. "It's so lovely to see you." She launched herself into his arms.

Brooke supposed this must be Angie. She was quite lovely to look at, her hair as raven black as her brother's and brushed in glowing waves down to her shoulders. She also had the same gray eyes as Jarrod, but whereas his were often cold and chilling hers were full of warmth and an underlying sense of mischief.

Angie was dressed much more informally than herself, in denims and a checked shirt. Very tall and slim, she carried herself with a self-confidence that was inborn; she turned from greeting her brother to appraise Brooke with curious eyes.

It wasn't a disapproving stare but nevertheless Brooke felt relieved that she was at least smartly dressed. She had gone out this morning and bought herself a new, casual day dress, packing an evening dress in case the Stones dressed for dinner. The day dress she had bought was a lemon and black flower print, fitted at her slim waist and finishing just below her knee.

She felt quite good in it and she met the younger girl's gaze unflinchingly, almost sighing her relief as Angie's face broke into a welcoming smile.

She came forward, her hand outstretched. "Hi, I'm Angie." She gave Jarrod a rueful look. "For once this brother of mine seems speechless." She grinned at him teasingly. "You must be in love."

He had a relaxed smile on his face. "It isn't a case of being in love, you just haven't stopped talking since you came out of the house."

Angie grimaced. "I hope he doesn't bully you like this."

Brooke laughed at her expression. "All the time, but I'm getting used to it."

"Surely not all the time. He seems to have taken time out to ask you to marry him." Angie put a friendly hand through the crook of Brooke's arm. "Can I see your ring?" she asked excitedly.

Brooke held out her hand for inspection, avoiding Jarrod's mocking gaze in her direction as his sister admired the ring. The two girls left him to bring in the small amount of luggage they had brought with them, Angie taking her into the lounge where the rest of the Stone family were waiting.

Brooke hung back in the doorway. Angie had proved to be just as nice as Jarrod had said she would be, but that didn't mean the rest of his family would be as welcoming. After all, Jarrod was an important man and his family would be expecting something a little bit special in his intended wife. The fact that it would never come to that wasn't important, they didn't know that.

"Little coward!" Jarrod muttered in her ear as he entered the room ahead of her, his firm grip on her wrist impelling her forward.

His taunt was enough to give her courage and she stood silently by his side as he greeted his family, making the introductions with practiced ease. First of all he introduced her to his mother, a small neat woman towered over by the rest of the family.

"At least I won't get a crick in my neck talking to you." Her gray eyes twinkled. "It's like living in the land of the giants," she explained.

She wasn't half as daunting as Brooke had expected her to be and she found herself smiling naturally, being made to feel as if she already belonged to this family. But she mustn't forget this was only a temporary arrangement, she mustn't become too involved. Never having had a family of her own she could find that all too easy.

Jarrod's father came next and it was obvious where his son got his looks from. His eyes might be the deep gray of his mother but the rest of him was all Clifford Stone. Tall and lean like his son, the black hair winged with gray at the temples, Cliffford Stone was still a very attractive man, although Brooke guessed he must be well into his sixties.

"Pleased to meet you, my dear." He bent to kiss her cheek warmly. "I'm glad to see that Jarrod has chosen wisely." He shook his son's hand.

"You're not at all what I expected," said the fourth and last member of the family. "The type of girl Jarrod usually goes around with—I expected you to be completely different.''

"David!" his father reprimanded sternly.

"How different?'' Brooke queried softly.

"Oh, you know, heavy perfume, so beautiful you almost don't look real, and so sophisticated it just isn't true," he grimaced.

Brooke looked at Jarrod, her eyes mocking him. "His taste must have changed."

"Definitely for the better," Dave said approvingly. "You've picked a real winner, Jarrod." He slapped his brother on the back. "Not that I'm sure you deserve her."

Jarrod grinned good-naturedly. "Oh, I'm sure Brooke thinks I deserve her."

"Definitely," she agreed firmly, his family not aware of their double-edged conversation.

"Would you like to take Brooke upstairs and show her her room," his mother suggested. "I've put her in the one next to yours," she informed him.

"Fine. Ready, darling?" he quirked one dark eyebrow at her.

"Yes," she replied huskily, the endearment embarrassing her.

Once upstairs in the room prepared for her Jarrod threw her case onto the bed before sitting down in the bedroom chair. It was a lovely room, beautifully furnished without losing any of its character, the gold and brown decor warm in appearance.

She cleared her throat nervously, ever conscious of Jarrod watching her through enigmatic eyes. "You have a nice family."

"And that surprised you." It was a statement not a question.

"A little," she admitted.

"They liked you, too, but then I knew they would. I have only one complaint."

"C-complaint?"

"Mmm." He looked thoughtfully at his wristwatch. "Your attitude toward me will have to improve. You jumped like a scared rabbit when I called you darling, and you studiously avoid calling me Jarrod."

"I've already explained why that is."

"Yes, but you can't just not call me anything."

"I find it easier that way," she said obstinately.

He stood up to leave. "Practice it to yourself while I freshen up. I'll just be next door when you're ready to go down to tea."

She unpacked her evening gown and denims so that the creases would fall out before she next wore them. She washed her face and freshened her makeup, feeling infinitely tidier when she had finished.

She hesitated about knocking on Jarrod's bedroom door, finally doing so with determination. She entered the room at his command to do so. That this had been his room since childhood was obvious from the pictures on the walls and the model airplanes suspended by string from the ceiling.

It was a nice room with a couple of pictures of Jarrod as a child on display on the dressing table. One of them had been taken when he was about twelve or thirteen, and already at that age he had the promise of the good looks that were now destructive to a woman's peace of mind.

She turned almost guiltily as she heard a movement behind her, her eyes widening with shock as she took in his bare chest and the way his trousers rested low down on his lean hips. It was impossible to look away from him as his muscles rippled as he dried himself with a thick fluffy towel. He must have just taken a shower and Brooke felt her cheeks color with embarrassment.

She dragged her eyes away from him with effort. "I'm sorry. I didn't realize you were...." She bit her lip nervously.

"I'm perfectly decent, Brooke," he taunted at her

hesitation. "Much more so than if I had just been swimming."

She moved awkwardly. "Yes, but this isn't a beach, and we...we're alone up here."

Jarrod threw the towel down onto the bed, shrugging his powerful shoulders into a black silk shirt and buttoning it with unhurried fingers. "You only have to make the slightest noise of protest and my mother and father would be up here like a shot." He tucked his shirt back into the waistband of his trousers. "They are the best chaperons you could ever wish to have."

"I'm sorry. It's just that—"

"You're a prude," he finished dryly. "It was only a bare chest, Brooke, nothing more. I was more than adequately dressed."

"It's just that I don't know you. You took me by surprise." She was making verbal excuses for her purely physical reaction to him. Her pulse had begun to beat erratically at the sight of him, her breathing constricted.

"I'll have to remember not to do it again until you know me better," he said sarcastically.

"There's no need to mock," she retorted crossly.

"Then don't be so damned stupid! You couldn't have been more shocked if I had been completely naked. You're twenty years of age, surely your life hasn't been that sheltered that a man with his shirt off can throw you into confusion? You must have had boyfriends in the past."

"A few," she admitted. "But none of them ever acted the way you do."

"All of them gentlemen, hmm?"

"Yes."

"Something we have already agreed I'm not."

"Yes," she said sharply. "If you're ready to go down, Mr. Stone, I—"

He grasped her wrist as she turned in preparation to

leave the room. "Jarrod!" he snapped savagely. "I thought I told you to call me Jarrod. If you can't manage a simple thing like that you're going to make complete fools out of both of us. Now say it! And manage to put a bit of feeling into it. Go on, say it!"

"Jarrod." It came out as a strangulated cry, his fingers painful on her wrist.

"Again," he ordered. "And say it properly this time."

"I...I can't. You're hurting me," she cried.

"Brooke!" he warned.

"All right, all right. But let go of my arm first." She sighed as he released her, rubbing the reddened skin. "You're a bully," she accused.

"You do seem to bring out those feelings in me," he agreed.

She pouted sulkily. "Jarrod," she said obediently, softly with feeling. How well his name rolled off the tongue, and how nice it sounded.

He grinned down at her. "Just try to keep it like that and they'll all believe you're in love with me."

"Jarrod," she repeated, looking up at him below lowered lashes, feeling more than usually shy with him alone in the intimacy of his bedroom.

To the girl entering the room at that moment they looked like a couple very much in love with each other, with Brooke gazing up into Jarrod's eyes and he grinning down at her, his expression softened.

"Am I intruding?" Angie asked mischievously.

Her brother turned to look at her. "Would it stop you if you were?"

She grinned. "No. I came to look for Brooke, and when she wasn't in her room I knew she must be in here with you..." she blushed as she realized what she had said. "What I mean is—"

Jarrod laughed at her embarrassment. "I think we know what you mean, Angie. Why were you looking for Brooke, as if I couldn't guess?" he grimaced.

She made a face at him. "I came to ask Brooke if she would like to see my studio, away from you oldies for a while."

"Minx!" He made a threatening step toward her, relenting as she looked set for flight. "What did mom say about your little idea?"

"She told me to wait until after tea."

"I agree with her."

Angie looked appealingly at Brooke. "Wouldn't you rather—"

"Tea first," Jarrod said firmly. "We've had quite a long drive here and we both need a drink and something to eat. No," he silenced her as she made to speak. "It can wait until later. Brooke?" He held out his hand to her.

She put her own hand into it, feeling the firm strength of his grasp. Among his family he was a different person, laughing and teasing, not at all the severe businessman she was used to seeing, and much less frightening.

THEY WERE a closely knit family, making Brooke feel like one of them. By the time tea was over she found herself feeling very much as if she had come home, and she felt guilty about these feelings. She was deceiving these kindly people, living a lie. She could only feel relieved when Angie renewed her suggestion that she might like to look at her studio.

"Of course, Jarrod is right," Angie said as she led the way up the stairs. "I'm not that good, but I do enjoy it, and I think I could make a career for myself in advertising."

"I'm sure Jarrod didn't—"

Angie laughed. "Oh, yes, he did. My brother is nothing if not honest." She threw open the door to her studio.

There were numerous sketches and paintings on the walls, all very good likenesses of her family. There was a half-finished portrait on the easel next to the window, but it was already clearly recognizable as Clifford Stone.

Brooke turned to look at the younger girl. "This is very good."

"Thank you, although it isn't very easy to get daddy to sit still. He may be retired but he's still very active. I have some sketches of Jarrod if you would like to see them?"

These sketches were in a separate portfolio, a few firm lines on paper showing Jarrod's strong face perfectly. "These are even better," Brooke said softly.

Angie grinned. "Jarrod refuses to sit still for five seconds, but he has such an arresting face that I just had to try and get him on paper. Handsome devil, isn't he?"

"Very," Brooke agreed unhesitant.

"He's kept you a big secret, you know. Mommy and daddy were very surprised when they saw yesterday's newspaper. They called Jarrod immediately and he confirmed that it was him. Where did you meet?"

She ought to have realized that Jarrod's sister would ask personal questions, but she hadn't, and now she wasn't ready for them. "We met at work," she answered evasively.

"And have you known him long?"

"About six months," she said truthfully.

Angie raised a surprised eyebrow. "I always knew Jarrod was clamlike about his friends but we've heard absolutely nothing about you. I suppose that proves just how serious he was about you."

Or more likely that he hadn't even known of her existence, which happened to be the truth. She quickly changed the subject, channeling it into something much less personal herself.

Dinner proved much less traumatic than she had imagined, too; seated next to Dave she was suitably entertained with the antics of his medical training.

Among all the hard work that went into the training Dave appeared to be having a lot of fun.

Brooke enjoyed his company, finding him much more approachable than Jarrod. He was younger for one thing, much less cynical and worldly. He looked like Jarrod in some ways, with his dark hair and powerful physique, but he had the laughing blue eyes of his father.

Jarrod came to sit beside her on the sofa as they drank their coffee in the lounge after dinner. "Stop flirting with my little brother," he warned her softly, a smile on his face for the other people in the room but a dangerous glitter in his eyes for her.

"Not so little," she muttered resentfully.

"Keep your sharp little claws out of him. You've managed to trick me into a phony engagement, don't try to get him into a real one. I wouldn't let him marry you, you know."

Her eyes glittered deeply violet. "A little premature, aren't you? We only met today."

"*We* only met yesterday—and we're engaged, now."

"Only temporarily," she said crossly.

"Right. So don't get any ideas about Dave. He has his life pretty well mapped out for the next few years, it doesn't include a wife."

Her eyes spat her dislike at him. "I don't intend marrying you or your brother."

"You may have to," he pointed out. "If our supposed wedding date is spread around too much."

"That doesn't mean I have to marry you. Playing your fiancée is something I don't mind doing, especially as I was the one who started all this, but marriage is a different matter." She put her empty coffee cup down on the table. "I think I would like to go to my room now, would your family mind?"

"It doesn't matter if I do?"

"No."

"Then go ahead," he told her grimly.

She stood up, excusing herself before leaving the room, closely followed by Jarrod. "Where are you going?" she demanded angrily. "To make sure I don't run away?"

He looked bored. "The idea never crossed my mind. I'm trying to look the part of the loving fiancé. Coming to your room for a long and passionate goodnight seemed to be called for."

Brooke gave him a scathing look before going determinedly up the stairs to her room. She hesitated at her bedroom door. "There's no need for you to come any farther."

Jarrod's look was taunting. "Frightened I might give you a repeat of last night?"

She blushed a fiery red. She had hoped he had forgotten last night, deliberately keeping off any subject herself that could bring that embarrassing interlude into the conversation. But it seemed Jarrod wasn't going to forget so easily. "Certainly not," she replied indignantly.

He watched her through narrowed eyes. "That was a punishment, you know."

She glared her dislike at him. "I never presumed it to be anything else," she snapped, going into the room and slamming the door behind her.

She leaned back against the door, her mouth set in a firm straight line. How dare he treat her like an impressionable child who had fallen in love with him! How dare he! Her shoulders slumped, he dared because until a few weeks ago that was exactly what she had been.

And now she found herself falling into that trap again. Jarrod was everything she had ever dreamed him to be and more. If only he weren't having an affair with a married woman!

CHAPTER FOUR

IT WAS HAPPENING again, that terrible nightmare that she couldn't escape from, that came to haunt her when she least expected it. She tossed restlessly around in the bed, anxious to free herself from the nightmare before it reached its terrifying climax, but knowing it would be impossible.

Tears streamed down her face as she witnessed once again with startling clarity the way her mother and father were laughing together, the sun shining down on them brightly as the three of them drove down to the coast for the day.

Her father hadn't seen the man driving at them on the wrong side of the road until it was too late, the screech of brakes amplified now in her dream, her mother's scream echoing time and time again in her brain. The car rolled over and over again until blackness took over and she woke up screaming.

Instantly the room was flooded with light, a tousled-haired, pajama-clad Jarrod rushing into the room. His face creased into a concerned frown as he saw her pale cheeks, the tears still flowing freely. He came swiftly to her side. "What's the matter? What happened?"

Brooke buried her face into his chest. "Oh, Jarrod, it was awful, awful!" she sobbed brokenly.

"What was?" he demanded, holding her against him.

"The dream...I had the dream again." The sobs were starting to cease now. "It's so long since it last happened I had almost forgotten about it."

His gray eyes were still darkened with concern as he held her at arm's length, searching her deathly white face for several long seconds. "What dream, Brooke?" he asked gently. "Tell me about it."

"I...I can't. I've never spoken to anyone about it."

"Tell me," he said persuasively. "After all, I was the one you cried out for."

Her eyes widened with disbelief. "You were?"

"Yes," he confirmed. "You called out my name several times before I got in here."

This surprised Brooke as she usually called her father's name. She looked worried. "Do you think I woke the rest of your family?"

"Well, no one has turned up yet, so I would say no. I only heard you because I was next door and I hadn't fallen asleep, yet. Look," he stood up. "If I pick you up and take you back to my room will you question my intentions?"

"No." She was shaking so much she just wanted to be back in his arms, held safe from that horrifying nightmare. She didn't want to stay in this room where the memory of that nightmare was so vivid.

He carried her to his room without another word, placing her gently between the sheets before getting in next to her, holding her against him with his arm around her shoulders, her head resting on his chest. "Now tell me about your dream, Brooke," he coaxed.

She shivered at the memory of it. "It was the accident, the accident that killed my parents. I saw it again—the crash, the way the car rolled over and over. I was unconscious before the car stopped turning."

"How old were you?"

"Five."

"And that's when you went to live with your aunt?"

"Yes. You see I was only kept in the hospital for

forty-eight hours and apparently the medical staff thought it better for my aunt to tell me of my parents' death in the comfort of her home, away from the clinical atmosphere. But she, my aunt, didn't care, she didn't care for my father, or the fact that he had married my mother. She . . . she woke me up the night I came out of the hospital to tell me they were both dead.''

Jarrod looked grim. "She woke you up to tell you that?''

She snuggled closer to him, repressing a shiver. "Yes,'' she admitted huskily. "Ever since then I've had these nightmares periodically. But the time between each one is getting longer and longer, this is the first one I've had for about a year.''

His arms tightened around her. "That woman had no right to have the care of a young child given to her.''

"She was kind enough in her own way, maybe hurting me was her way of showing her grief.''

He reached out his hand and switched off the light, instantly putting the room into darkness. "Go to sleep now, Brooke. You're quite safe, I'm here with you.''

"But I . . . I can't stay here.''

His warm breath ruffled the hair at her temple. "You aren't going back into that room on your own. You're obviously still upset. You'll stay here with me. Go to sleep now, I'll stay awake until I know you're asleep.''

"Thank you.''

She felt his lips at her temple and her feelings changed to something quite different from fear. She was here in Jarrod Stone's bed being held in his arms. It was still frightening, but fear of another kind.

"Go to sleep, Brooke,'' he ordered abruptly. "And stop letting your imagination run riot. I think you've had enough of an upset for one night, so let me assure you I have no intention of doing anything to upset you any more. We can talk again in the morning.''

Brooke didn't think she could possibly sleep held in his arms like this, but the even rise and fall of his chest soon lulled her into a false sense of security, and within minutes she was asleep.

She woke slowly the next morning, wondering where she could possibly be. Then she remembered, looking down at the dark head resting on her breasts— Jarrod Stone still very much asleep. His arm rested around her waist, his body molded to her side.

She could just see the angle of his face, softened now in sleep. He looked younger but just as handsome. And she had slept in his bed with him all night! She was sure that none of his friends would believe that they had spent the last few hours together in this bed and he hadn't made one single pass at her. She wasn't sure she believed it herself. With his reputation she would have expected something quite different, maybe she was even a little disappointed.

But she didn't have time to puzzle over that because at that moment someone came unannounced into the bedroom. Brooke felt her heart sink as she recognized Angie, an Angie who hadn't seen her yet because she was preoccupied with fastening her wristwatch to her arm.

"Come on, Jarrod. It's..." her voice trailed off as she saw Brooke cradled in her brother's arms, her cheeks coloring a fiery red. "Oh, dear, what have I done now," she groaned. "I didn't mean to—"

"You haven't," Brooke said firmly, gently shaking Jarrod to wake him up. "I...we...."

"Hey, come on, Jarrod. You can't...." Dave too, stood transfixed in the doorway. He took Angie's arms, pulling her out of the door. "Excuse us, Brooke. We didn't realize." With a cheeky grin he closed the door behind them.

She shook Jarrod more forcefully. "Wake up, will you?" she demanded. "Jarrod! Wake up."

He lay on his back, stretching his arms above his

head. "Mmm," he groaned. "What time is it?" He looked at her with sleepy eyes.

"Never mind the time," she retorted crossly. "We've just had visitors."

"Really?" he asked disinterestedly, turning on his side to look at the clock on the side table. "Angie or Dave?"

"Both. But how did you know?" she frowned.

He shrugged, pushing back the bedclothes to get out of bed. He stretched again. "It's a bit cramped in there for two people."

"How did you know it was either your sister or your brother?" she repeated to cover her embarrassment.

"Because it's after seven-thirty and when I'm home we always go for a horseback ride at seven-fifteen. Obviously they thought I had slept in and they had come to wake me."

"Oh, obviously," she said dryly. "Don't you care that they saw us together in this bed—and drew their own conclusions?"

He raised his eyebrows. "What's the point of worrying about it. I'm sure that by now Angie has rushed in and told my mother, too."

"Oh, no!" she paled. "I couldn't bear it. And I certainly couldn't face your mother and father again if they have been told."

He pulled a clean shirt out of the wardrobe. "Why not? They probably think we sleep together, anyway. A lot of engaged couples do nowadays."

"I wouldn't, and especially not with you. You're the sort that would take advantage of the engagement and forget about the marriage."

"With you I may not be allowed to. My mother and father won't simply accept the end of our engagement in a couple of months' time, not after this morning. We may just have to get married to satisfy them."

She gave him a puzzled look. "You're very calm about it."

He stripped off his pajama jacket, his torso rippling with muscle. "What else do you expect me to be?"

Brooke sat up in the bed, uncaring of the inadequacy of her cotton nightdress. "I expect you to be angry at perhaps having to marry someone you don't love."

"But you do see it may be a possibility?"

Remembering the looks she had received from Angie and Dave and the kindness Mr. and Mrs. Stone had shown her she knew that it could happen. They were Jarrod's family, and no matter how he may behave away from home, here he behaved like any normal son would to his parents, with respect and love. Besides, she couldn't bear for them to think badly of her.

"Yes," she acknowledged softly.

"I'm no happier about it than you are," he snapped, picking up the sound of finality in her voice.

"Then why don't you get angry, shout a little?"

He walked to the bathroom door, his fresh clothing in his hand, clothed only in the silk pajama trousers that rested low down on his narrow hips, showing clearly the strength and power of his body. "Being married to you may not be so bad, you felt quite good in my arms last night, and when I kissed you on Friday I wouldn't say we disliked each other."

"You mean.." she paused for breath. "You mean you would expect...expect a normal marriage?"

He gave a mocking smile. "You've been reading too many romantic novels. Marriages of convenience don't happen nowadays, or if they do they certainly have a physical side. I wouldn't marry any woman just to look at her," he scorned.

"But it *would* be very convenient for you, wouldn't it?" she queried softly.

Gray eyes narrowed to steely slits. "Would it?"

"Oh, yes," she scorned. "A newly married man would hardly be suspected of having an affair with another man's wife."

"And who would that be?" he asked tauntingly.

"You know very well who I mean," she said tartly.

"The beautiful Selina," he replied unhesitantly.

"Exactly."

"Mmm, you could be right," he said thoughtfully.

"I wouldn't stand for that if I were your wife. I couldn't condone you having an affair with that woman. I didn't even like her."

"Oh, I see, if you had liked her it would have been a different matter."

"Don't be ridiculous. And I certainly wouldn't be your real wife. I may have been reading too many romantic novels but I think I prefer the way they turn out."

"You do?" he looked surprised. "But they usually end up with the hero and the heroine in each other's arms, don't they?"

"Well, yes, but...we won't! And that's why you aren't ever going to make love to me. I happen to believe that sort of thing should only happen between people who love each other."

"And you don't think you could ever love me?"

"Never!" She couldn't meet his probing eyes in case he should see her lie. He was much too astute to miss the love shining in her eyes for him.

"Then that's too bad because I have no intention of having a wife just to put her in a glass case. Women are for loving and—"

"And you love them," she finished bitchily.

"Yes."

"God, you're such a—"

"I warned you once before about calling me names." His eyes glittered dangerously.

"If the cap fits..." she said pointedly.

He laughed softly. "I'll see you at breakfast. I'm going for that horseback ride now. If I were you I'd try to get a little more sleep, it may improve your temper."

His laughter still echoed in the room long after he

had left it. Brooke threw one of the pillows at the closed bathroom door. Damn the man! Damn the arrogance of him.

She went back to her own room, how could she be expected to sleep in his bed after what had happened to her this morning. She still blushed at the thought of Angie coming into the room and finding her in Jarrod's arms. Whatever must she have thought? What a damned stupid question, it must be obvious what she had thought, what the whole family would think when they knew.

And she had to face them all, probably at breakfast. Not that she was hungry, but she knew the dreaded moment had to be faced sometime, and she would rather it was sooner than later. Besides, she knew Jarrod wouldn't let her cower in her room all day.

If only he weren't so damned calm about the whole thing. It didn't seem to bother him that his young sister had walked into his bedroom and found them in a compromising situation. And then he also had the nerve to say they would have to get married and that he would expect the marriage to be a real one.

He had already called the tune far too many times in a situation that she herself had created, and she wasn't about to let any man make love to her simply because he considered it his right to do so. Oh, no, Mr. Jarrod Stone had pushed her about far too much already, she wasn't about to marry him, too.

Only his mother was in the dining room when she came down to breakfast at eight-thirty, the others obviously not back from their ride yet. She accepted the cup of coffee Sarah Stone had poured out for her, sipping the scalding liquid in an effort not to look at the other woman—her embarrassment too acute.

"Have the two of you discussed a wedding date?" Jarrod's mother asked softly.

Brooke's cheeks flamed. No preliminaries, but

straight to the point! "Not really. Look, Mrs. Stone, I—"

"Call me Sarah, please," she invited graciously. "And I hope that when you know me better you'll call me mother like my other children do."

Everything this woman said made her feel more and more guilty for her deceit. Her last words made her feel choked with emotion, never having had anyone she could call mother. And Sarah Stone was exactly the type of mother she would have liked herself, loving and concerned for her children but not interfering.

"Thank you," she accepted huskily. "But I want you to know that what Angie saw this morning was not as it seemed. Jarrod and I hadn't...well, we hadn't...."

Sarah smiled gently, patting Brooke's hand reassuringly. "I know that, my dear. Jarrod has already explained to me what happened and I think he did the right thing. It wouldn't have been right to leave you on your own after such a horrible experience. Jarrod did the only thing possible."

"Jarrod told you?" she repeated huskily.

"My son is a very forthright person, if he had been making love to you he would have told me that, too '

"Oh."

"You mustn't mind us, Brooke. We aren't a family that likes to have secrets, although my eldest son rather surprised us with this engagement."

"It was all rather sudden," Brooke excused.

"So he explained, and the press do have a way of finding out these things when you don't want them to. Jarrod explained that the engagement wasn't to be officially announced until your birthday on Tuesday, but as the press had already announced it to the world you decided to go ahead with it now. These newspapermen can be so annoying at times," she tutted.

Her birthday on Tuesday! How on earth had Jarrod

known about that? Of course, her file. And he had used that knowledge to his advantage. But then that was probably how he had got to be the successful businessman he was today, by remembering things and using them when the opportunity arose. Well, he was certainly using her to his greatest advantage, hiding his affair with this phony engagement.

"Yes," she agreed quietly, helping herself to a slice of toast.

"I want you to know that Clifford and I would like to arrange for the wedding to take place from here. I hope you'll allow us that pleasure."

Brooke blushed once more. "I...well, I...we haven't really...."

Jarrod came in at that moment—tall, lithe and attractive in a black polo-necked sweater and fitted cream trousers. He bent to kiss his mother's cheek. "Good morning, mother." He grinned down mockingly at Brooke before kissing her, too, on the lips. "Good morning again, my love," he drawled, sitting down next to her.

"Good morning," she mumbled.

His mother beamed at the two of them, unaware of the tension between them. "I was just explaining to Brooke that your father and I would like the wedding to take place from here, to arrange it all for you both."

Jarrod raised one dark eyebrow. "You've been discussing the wedding?"

"No, I—"

"Not Brooke, no," his mother laughed. "Just me. I'm so excited about having a wedding in the family at last that I can't seem to stop talking about it. I wondered if you had decided on a definite date, yet?"

"Not really," he sipped his coffee. "Next month has been mentioned, but we—"

"Next month!" his mother gasped. "But that's much too soon. I couldn't possibly get everything arranged in so short a time, and Brooke will have so much shopping to do. And you can't possibly live in that apartment of yours; you'll have to look for a suitable house."

"Calm down," Jarrod laughed. "I only said next month had been mentioned, not that it had been decided upon."

Brooke's mouth tightened at the mockery in his eyes for her. Next month had been mentioned, by her to Selina Howard, and he wouldn't let her forget it.

Sarah Stone sighed her relief. "Stop teasing me, Jarrod. So you haven't decided when the wedding is to be?"

"Not really." He sat back in his chair. "We've only just got engaged, mom, I think that's enough commitment for the time being. Besides, Brooke needs time to adjust to having a family and time to adjust to me."

His mother stood up to leave the table. "I'll just go and talk to the cook about dinner." She stopped next to Brooke's chair. "I hope you don't feel that I'm trying to rush you into anything. Jarrod's right, you need time. I'm sorry."

Brooke gave a shy smile. "You have nothing to apologize for."

"Thank you."

She turned on Jarrod once they were alone. "Did you have to do that, embarrass your mother in that way?"

He looked at her calmly. "What would you have had me do, agree to everything she suggested? I thought you said you didn't want to marry me."

"I don't. I wouldn't marry you under any circumstances."

"My, my, my," murmured Dave from behind them. "You've only been engaged two days, I think you ought to give Jarrod a little longer than that."

Brooke paled even more, the strain she had been living under the last two days coming to the fore. She stood up with a scraping of the chair. "Excuse me," she muttered before dashing out of the room.

She didn't care where she went, all she knew was that she had to get away from Jarrod and the way he kept taunting her. Was he going to punish her forever!

She rushed out of the house, answering Angie's greeting as she came in, her smile vague, before running off in the direction of the woods to the right of the house.

Finally she stopped running, dropping down into the undergrowth in utter exhaustion. What would Dave think of her statement? What could he think— she had made an absolute fool of herself. But Jarrod would keep goading her, taunting her until she had to retaliate.

But at other times he could be quite thoughtful, helping her out of a situation when it became too complicated for her to handle. But he hadn't helped her this time, he had just made things worse.

She wasn't really surprised when she heard someone else moving around in the denseness of the wood, obviously Jarrod's family would pressure him into coming to look for her. She made no attempt to move, not even looking up when she knew he was standing directly in front of her, his firm muscled thighs clearly outlined in the cream trousers.

He sank down in the grass beside her. "That was a bit stupid, wasn't it," he said softly.

Brooke was clutching at the long grass as if for support, unnerved by his closeness. Her cheeks were still wet with tears. "I couldn't...couldn't think what to do. What did...did you tell Dave?"

Jarrod lay back in the grass, his arms behind his head as he gazed up at the blue sky through the tree-tops. "I just told him that you were still embarrassed about this morning; that you were so upset about it you refused to marry me."

"And did he believe you?"

He turned to look at her. "Why shouldn't he, you *were* embarrassed about it."

"But that wasn't the reason I said I wouldn't marry you."

"No," he agreed, sitting up to gently touch her cheek. "You did that because once again I pushed you too far. I'm sorry."

Her eyes widened, her senses reeling at the touch of his hand on her cheek. "You're...you're sorry?"

His eyes deepened in color as his gaze rested on her parted lips. "Yes, Brooke..." he murmured throatily, bending his head to claim her lips. "Brooke!" he gasped, gently lowering her back into the undergrowth, his body pressed urgently to her side.

She hadn't been expecting this onslaught, responding without thought. His mouth was sure and experienced, reducing her to a quivering mass in his arms, his body firm and demanding on hers.

His mouth left hers to travel down the column of her throat to the hollow between her breasts, her nipples clearly visible through the lime green vest top she had chosen to wear with matching trousers. His lips evoked a response wherever they touched, soft and caressing and totally in control.

Brooke's fingers were entwined in the darkness of his hair, inciting him on to further caresses. It was peaceful here, the only noises ones of the birds and the soft rustle of the leaves in the trees. They were in a world apart, a world without time or meaning. And Jarrod was kissing her as if he really enjoyed doing it, drawing a response from her but not demanding one.

As his lips burned across her throat she kissed the strong angle of his jawbone, aware of the tangy smell of his after-shave and the slight roughness of his skin. His hands moved with certainty across her waist to trail a path of fire up to her shoulders, smoothing the hollows of her throat with impatient fingers.

Brooke was aflame with longing, longing for Jarrod's possession of her. She had never felt this way in any other man's arms, never responded so totally to the senses. If he chose to take her now she wouldn't raise a single objection, would give herself up to just being made his.

He drew back his head, his eyes a deep aroused gray, his own breathing as labored as her own. "I want you, you know that, don't you," his voice was husky, his tone one of passionate intensity.

"Yes." She was mesmerized by the look in his eyes.

"Do you mind?"

"Do you?"

He shook his head in the negative. "At the moment I don't mind a thing, except perhaps that this isn't exactly the ideal place for this sort of thing."

Brooke gave him a dreamy smile, caressing his furrowed brow with great daring. "I think it's just perfect."

He gave a husky chuckle. "Someone may come along," he pointed out reasonably.

Her hands were slowly pulling his head back down to her. "They won't," she murmured against his lips. "They wouldn't dare."

With a groan his mouth took possession of hers once again, less gentle now and more demanding. Their hearts beat as one, the rest of their bodies crying out for the same thing. They both knew what they wanted and there was no holding back, on either side.

Her hands caressed and touched his muscled back beneath his sweater, his skin firm and smooth, all of him totally male. His lips played with hers until she rose up to meet him, lying on top of him now, she the one doing the kissing.

Jarrod's hands moved across her back to the waistband of her trousers, pulling her vest top free so that he could touch the heated skin beneath. She shivered at his hands upon her body, lifting her head to look at him.

Even lying beneath her like this he was still the master, arousing her with just the look in his eyes. "What's wrong?" he asked softly. "Changed your mind?"

She shook her head wordlessly, knowing that she was irrevocably in love with this man. She had known it last night when she had woken up to scream his name. Always in the past she had called for her father, sobbing for him until she had almost made herself ill, but last night she had cried out for Jarrod, for the man who now meant everything to her.

"Then come back here," he demanded throatily, once again bending over her to press upon her those soul-destroying kisses that made a mockery of will-power.

She responded passionately, as she knew she always would in this man's arms. One of his hands moved to cup her breast and she felt him shudder against her.

"God, you're naked underneath this top!" he groaned against her lips.

"I know," she answered happily.

"Oh, God, Brooke, how do you expect me to have any control with you dressed like this? I can't—"

"Ssh," she silenced him swiftly. "Someone's coming through the woods toward us." She could hear the snapping of twigs as whoever it was came closer and closer to them.

Jarrod swung away from her. "Oh, hell!" he swore angrily, his expression grim. "It just has to be Angie or Dave, it just has to be! Only they would dare." He was proved correct when a few seconds later Dave emerged out of the trees. "What was that you were saying about they wouldn't dare?" he muttered, standing up to brush the leaves off his trousers. He turned to pull her to her feet. "My family dare anything, you'll learn that in time."

The scowl he gave Dave was evidence of his displeasure and Dave wasn't insensitive to his mood. "Did I arrive at the wrong time again?" he asked innocently.

"Completely the wrong time." Jarrod brushed past him on his way back to the house, anger in every line of his rigidly held body.

Dave shrugged helplessly at Brooke as his brother marched off. "I'm sorry."

She brushed the grass from her trousers to cover her embarrassment. "That's all right." She made to follow Jarrod but Dave's hand on her arm stopped her.

"I really mean it, Brooke. I didn't mean to interrupt." He looked as embarrassed as she did.

"You didn't interrupt anything." On top of her embarrassment she had the hurt that Jarrod could walk away and leave her like this.

Dave followed her gaze as she watched Jarrod's fast disappearing figure. "I shouldn't worry about Jarrod. If he hadn't left when he did he would probably have hit me. I've seen him mad in the past but never that mad." He whistled between his teeth.

Brooke tried her hardest to regain her composure. "You'll have to blame me for that. I had rather a silly argument with him."

He nodded. "And I came along and interrupted you making up your argument."

"Not really, you just came along at the wrong time and said the wrong thing." She gave a light laugh. "I suppose I'm just feeling particularly sensitive at the moment."

"They tell me it isn't easy being engaged."

"After two days?" she teased.

"Well, Jarrod's a pretty arrogant man and very overpowering. Considering the way he rushed to protect your name with my mother this morning I would say you aren't sleeping together, yet. That can make things rather tense."

Brooke's eyes widened at his forthright attitude.
"I—"

"I'm too honest for you, hmm?" He guessed the
reason for her hesitation.

"Blunt, I would say," she agreed huskily.

"But right," he grinned. "Jarrod's really strung up
about you."

"I don't think—"

"Oh, but he is." Dave fell into step beside her as
she began to make her way across the grounds. "I
guess you're the type of girl men marry, and Jarrod
isn't used to waiting. Besides, he isn't getting any
younger."

She burst out laughing. "I don't think he would say
thank you for saying that."

"Neither do I," he chuckled. "But mom's over the
moon about the wedding. She'd just about given up
on Jarrod, we all had. He never seemed to have the
same girl friend longer than a few weeks, and he
never brought any of them home."

"Perhaps, they weren't the sort of girl he could
bring home."

"You could be right, in fact you probably are. Are
you coming into the house now? I promise not to say
anything too outrageous for the rest of the day."

She couldn't help smiling at the "little boy look"
on his face. "I think I'll go for a walk, get myself an
appetite for lunch."

"Okay." He gave a friendly salute before leaving
her.

Brooke wandered around the well-kept grounds for
well over an hour. It was a beautiful estate, really well
cared for. It must take an army of gardeners to care
for a place this size, and even more staff to run the
house itself.

It made her all the more aware of the difference in
background between Jarrod and herself. He had been
brought up in the lap of luxury, surrounded by his

family who loved him, whereas she had been brought up by an aunt who hated her, and who begrudged every penny she had to spend on her.

She would never fit into this sort of background, so perhaps it was as well that their engagement wasn't a real one. She could cope with a weekend but anything else would be out of the question. But there never would be anything else, this engagement would end as soon as she could make it possible.

Lunch was a pleasant family affair but Brooke fell in readily with Jarrod's suggestion that they leave midafternoon. His family protested strongly, but he was adamant, managing their departure with consummate ease.

"You'd had enough, hadn't you?" he remarked as they drove out of the driveway.

She sighed. "Was it that obvious?"

"Only to me." His narrowed eyes remained on the road.

"You didn't have to leave because of me," she said stiffly. "I was fine."

"You were getting jumpy. You could have said something that would have landed us in a lot of trouble."

"I see. I'm sorry," she said shortly, angry with him and herself; angry with him because he was right and angry with herself for letting him get under her skin in this way. But she couldn't forget what had happened between them this morning, most of all, she didn't want to forget.

Jarrod had been very cool toward her when they had met again, treating her to a strained politeness solely for the benefit of his family. But his attitude had only made her more tense. He was right, of course, if they hadn't left when they had she would have exploded, with repercussions for both of them.

"No need to apologize," he told her abruptly. "I realize I'm to blame for your tension. But damn it!"

he swore savagely. "You didn't resist me, you invited me even."

Brooke was taken aback by this attack on her. "There's nothing wrong with letting a man kiss you," she answered hotly. "You may consider me young but I'm not that inexperienced."

"I think you already proved that," he said dryly.

"What do you mean?" she frowned.

He gave a harsh laugh. "You know all the right moves, don't you, all the little tricks to turn a man on."

She gasped, angered and hurt by what he was saying to her. She may have made all the right moves, but only with Jarrod had she ever come sensually alive, liking him to touch her and to touch him in return. But he was making it sound like something it wasn't, making *her* sound like something she wasn't and never could be.

"It would appear so," she said chillingly, "if I could manage to turn *you* on. With all your experience with women that can't be too easy."

"Right," he agreed grimly, obviously not liking what she said.

"If you can't take it don't dish it out," she returned swiftly.

"Oh, I can take it, but from you I don't intend to take anything, not your body or your sarcasm."

"The first you won't get a chance at and the second you shouldn't evoke."

"I'll try to remember that," he said coldly. "You would do well to do the same."

"Oh, go to hell!"

The silence during the rest of the journey was very oppressive and Brooke for one was glad when he stopped the car outside her apartment. She hesitated. "Would you...would you like to come in for coffee?" she invited, more out of politeness than a genuine wish for his company.

"No thanks," he replied curtly, getting her case out of the back of the car before opening her car door for her to get out.

"It's early, yet!"

"Good night, Brooke," he said firmly. "I'll call you tomorrow." His gray eyes raked over her with chilling intensity. "I have a dinner appointment this evening," he added coldly.

Brooke's eyes sharpened. "With Selina Howard?"

His smile was cruel. "Who else?"

CHAPTER FIVE

"You're very quiet today," Jean said softly.

Brooke forced herself to take an interest in what Jean was saying. "Sorry?"

"I said you're very quiet. You've been like this all day, and yesterday, too. Is there anything wrong?"

Anything wrong! She hadn't heard from Jarrod since their parting Sunday evening—that was what was wrong. He had said he would call her but she knew for a fact that he had flown to Paris for the day yesterday. But he had no excuse for today. And he was definitely upstairs in his office.

"Brooke?" Jean prompted.

She gave a vague smile. "Sorry. No, there's nothing wrong."

"Sure?"

"Yes."

"I didn't know if perhaps something had happened over the weekend. It must have been quite nerve-racking to meet Mr. Stone's family. I would have been terrified myself."

"They were all very nice," she said dully. Why hadn't Jarrod called her? It was her birthday today and he hadn't even remembered. He could remember it for the benefit of his family but he hadn't even had the courtesy to send her a card.

"You don't sound very enthusiastic."

"They really were," Brooke insisted. "Although as you say, I was a bit nervous. But they did make me very welcome."

Jean sighed as her telephone exchange began to buzz again, but it left Brooke to sink into the misery of her thoughts. In just two days Jarrod had worked his way into her heart and become the most important person in her life. And she felt lost without any contact from him, with no word from him at all.

He had already been up in his office when she had arrived at a quarter to nine this morning and he hadn't yet come down for lunch. She was hesitating about going to lunch herself in the hope that she might see him.

By the time two-thirty came around she had come to the conclusion that he wasn't leaving for lunch and by this time she really had no enthusiasm for eating herself. It was as if Jarrod was deliberately avoiding her. But that couldn't be so, he didn't consider her important enough to go to that extreme.

She wandered home alone at five-thirty, still unable to find any appetite when she saw the makings of the chicken salad she had left in the refrigerator for her dinner. It was miserable having to spend her birthday alone, although she knew it didn't have to be that way; one of her friends would have come out with her. But tonight she wasn't fit company for anyone. Oh, damn Jarrod, damn and blast him.

She moped around the apartment for half an hour or more, picking things up before putting them down disinterestedly again. Her twenty-first birthday and she was spending it alone. Not even her friends at work had remembered.

Finally, through boredom, she washed and curled her hair. That wasted at least an hour for her. Oh, she was so bored, only seven-thirty and already she had no way left to fill her evening.

The ringing of the doorbell seemed a welcome interruption to her loneliness and she rushed to answer the door before whoever it was went away again. But apparently they had no such intention, the doorbell ringing again as she reached for the doorknob

She wrenched it open, staring openmouthed at Jarrod as he stood on her doorstep. "Jarrod," she murmured wonderingly, completely overwhelmed by how handsome he looked.

He looked devastatingly attractive, the wine-colored velvet jacket fitting smoothly across his shoulders, the black trousers molded to his firm muscular thighs, and the velvet bow tie matched the color of his jacket perfectly and emphasized the snowy whiteness of the silk shirt he wore.

Brooke's breath had caught and held in her throat at the sight of him, and even though she felt slightly ridiculous standing here unable to say anything she just couldn't force a word past her lips. It was the complete unexpectedness of his appearance here that had unnerved her the most.

Jarrod quirked a mocking eyebrow. "Are you going to keep me standing here all evening or do you think I might possibly come inside?"

"Oh...oh, sorry," she blushingly opened the door. "Come in, by all means."

He strolled into her cheaply furnished but clean lounge and Brooke followed him, feeling much too casually dressed in her denims and vest top against his sophisticated elegance. She watched as he sat down on the sofa, placing a huge white box down next to him. The box looked familiar and she remembered he had given her one like it before.

She twisted her hands together nervously. "Why are you here?" she asked bluntly, curiosity getting the better of good manners.

"I am your fiancé," he pointed out.

"That hasn't seemed to bother you for the last two days," she said bitchily.

"Are you angry about something?" He watched her through narrowed eyes.

"Angry!" Brooke repeated sharply. "What do I

have to be angry about? What *right* do I have to be angry about anything?''

"You tell me," he said mildly, too mildly.

"You said you would call me," she reminded accusingly.

"And now I'm here instead."

"Two days later."

His mouth tightened. "I was out of the country yesterday."

"I know that."

"Then you also know the reason I didn't call you. Use your common sense, Brooke, I was away on business, I didn't have time to make personal calls."

"Not to me, anyway," she muttered. "I'm sure some of your other—acquaintances didn't merit the same casualness." She didn't need to mention Selina Howard's name, he would know very well who she meant.

Jarrod looked impatient. "What's the matter with you?" he demanded. "I'm sure the fact that I haven't called you hasn't been enough to put you in this mood. You couldn't give a damn about me and you know it."

"I care about the fact that I look pretty stupid when I can't even say when I'm seeing you again. You're the owner of Stone Computers, and as you can imagine we gained quite a lot of attention by getting engaged. I'm asked questions about you all day and I simply have no answers."

"It's none of their damned business, anyway," he declared arrogantly. "I don't care to have my personal affairs discussed with them."

She gave a harsh laugh. "Then maybe you shouldn't cause so much gossip."

His eyes snapped angrily, icy gray in color. "May I remind you that you started this charade, not I, and consequently caused the gossip!"

"But I didn't start the rumors about you and Mrs. Howard, your so-called friends did that." She allowed her hurt and disappointment to come out, hurt and disappointment that no one had remembered her birthday. But then that wasn't Jarrod's fault, he had no reason to remember it.

"I didn't come here to argue with you," he said reasonably. "But I think you would be well-advised not to listen to rumors. They so often turn out to have no foundation."

She gave him a scathing look. "Are you trying to say your friends were wrong?"

"I'm sure the two women you heard talking weren't friends of mine."

"But they would like to be," she scorned.

He stood up forcefully. "For God's sake what's the matter with you! I came over here to—"

"Yes?" she cut in rudely. "Just why did you come here? Dressed like that I would assume you're going out somewhere."

He nodded. "You would assume correct."

Brooke turned away. "Don't let me keep you," she said stiffly.

"Oh, hell!" He ran an agitated hand through his thick dark hair. "You are keeping me, I came here to take you out."

"Why?" she asked suspiciously.

"Does there have to be a reason?"

"Oh, yes, there has to be a reason. Who do you want to parade me in front of this time?"

He sighed heavily, picking up the box he had brought with him and handing it to her. "Put this on and I'll show you."

Brooke looked down at the box as if he had physically struck her with it, knowing it had to be some form of clothing in a box of that name. "What is it?"

He pushed it toward her. "Open it and see," he encouraged.

Like most people, Brooke had a natural curiosity and she reluctantly took the box, ripping off the lid to sort through the tissue paper inside. Nestling among the paper was a silky gown, dazzlingly white in color. She pulled it out with shaking hands, holding it against her.

It was a beautiful gown, Grecian in style, and Brooke loved it on sight. She looked at Jarrod over its silky folds. "For me?" she breathed softly.

He gave a soft throaty chuckle. "Well, it isn't for me."

She blushed. "I know that, but I— *Why* is it for me?" She was still hoping he had remembered her birthday.

"Just put it on and then we'll go out."

"But I—"

"Brooke!" he said warningly. "Go and change."

She hurried quickly to her room, anxious to do as he said. She rushed into the bathroom, washing quickly before applying a light makeup. Thank goodness she had washed her hair earlier, the red lights very pronounced.

The gown fitted her perfectly and she could only wonder at Jarrod's correct assessment of her size. That certainly hadn't been in her file! The gown had a plunging neckline, making it impossible for her to wear a bra and she felt slightly self-conscious as she saw how her breasts were emphasized under the thin material.

She felt even more so a few minutes later as Jarrod's gray eyes roamed freely over her body, lingering slightly on her firm uptilted breasts. She looked back at him below lowered lashes, longing for his approval.

"Do you like the gown?" He watched her closely.

She smiled shyly. "Do you?"

His eyes darkened. "You look beautiful in it."

"Thank you. You have excellent taste. I would never have bought a gown in this style for myself."

"That's a shame, because you have the perfect figure for it." He looked at his wristwatch. "We have to go now, Brooke."

She collected the velvet wrap he had given her the last time they had gone out for the evening. "I . . ." she hesitated. "I don't like you to keep buying me things."

"If you look good in them what does it matter who bought them." He took the familiar flat jewelry case out of his pocket. "I want you to wear these, too." He held out the necklace and earrings she had insisted he keep.

Brooke attached the earrings, bending forward as Jarrod fixed the clasp of her necklace. She liked the feel of his firm sure fingers against her skin, and the memory of the way he kissed her on Sunday came all too vividly into her mind.

She moved away from him jerkily. "We must be going somewhere important if you want me to wear all this finery. I would look decidedly out of place in a restaurant or somewhere equally as casual."

"We're going to a party," he told her shortly. "And we're already late."

"I suppose it will go on for hours, yet—most parties do."

"Possibly," he nodded distantly. "Ready?"

"Yes," she agreed huskily.

They drove to one of the largest hotels in town and Brooke looked at Jarrod interestedly. "The party is here?"

He turned to look at her. "Yes, in one of the smaller reception rooms."

Once outside the car she hung back, nervous about meeting Jarrod's friends for a second time. But his possessive hold on her arm impelled her forward. He opened the door for her, ushering her inside. They found themselves in a small cloakroom area where her wrap was taken by the young man obviously there for just such a purpose. The room behind the double doors was surprisingly quiet for a party.

"Are we the only ones here?" she whispered to Jarrod.

He grinned at her, moving forward to throw open the double doors. Instantly the feeling of quiet disappeared, people shouting "Surprise!" from every corner of the room. And they were talking to her!

Jarrod bent his head to kiss her fleetingly on the lips. "Happy birthday, Brooke."

She looked from him to his family, all the girls she knew at work, and a few other people who were probably his own personal friends, tears gathering in her violet blue eyes. "You hadn't forgotten," she choked. "I thought everyone had forgotten "

"They had all been sworn to secrecy," he corrected. "It took quite a lot of organizing to get everyone here at such short notice." He lowered his voice. "It can be quite difficult to do when you've only known for four days about the birthday."

She looked up at him mischievously. "You've only known *me* four days."

"True," he chuckled.

Without hesitating she threw her arms around his neck, kissing him enthusiastically before her attention was taken by the guests he had invited for her. She received all the presents and cards that had been sadly lacking this morning, loving them all, but the present she liked most came from Jarrod's sister Angie. It was a portrait of Jarrod, a very good portrait that she would treasure as long as she lived. A portrait of the man she loved.

Jarrod grimaced as she put it in the place of honor among her other gifts. "Angie!" he guessed with feeling. "She could have thought of something a little more original than that."

Brooke looked at it admiringly, a slight curve to her soft pink lips. "I think it's just perfect."

"Hardly perfect," he denied. "I'm sure I don't

have quite that physique. She's made me out to be some sort of Adonis.''

"It's beautiful," Brooke insisted.

"God, now I'm really insulted."

"Surely Brooke isn't insulting you, darling," drawled a familiar husky voice. "Sorry we're late, Jarrod, but Charles's flight was delayed."

Brooke quickly masked her displeasure at Selina Howard being invited here to her party, turning to smile at the other woman politely. But Selina Howard wasn't looking at her, her eyes for Jarrod alone, slanting green eyes that devoured him at a glance.

Brooke found that look frankly disgusting, especially as the man at her side was instantly recognizable as Charles Howard, her husband. He was a tall distinguished man with a handsomeness that was almost as breathtaking as Jarrod's. Selina Howard must indeed be greedy to possess a husband and lover with such virility.

Charles Howard put out his hand. "Nice to see you again, Jarrod," he smiled. "As Selina has already said, my flight was delayed, hence our lateness."

"I'm pleased you could come at all. You must be tired after your flight." Jarrod moved to put a possessive arm around Brooke's shoulders. "My fiancée, Brooke Faulkner."

"Happy birthday, my dear," Charles said smoothly. "You don't know how much pleasure it gives me to see Jarrod joining us other poor downtrodden devils."

She laughed, noting his twinkling blue eyes. "He hasn't, yet—an engagement isn't necessarily a marriage."

"But you did say the marriage was to be next month," Selina Howard spoke to her for the first time. "All of Jarrod's friends are waiting in anticipation of their invitation. Have you decided on the actual date, yet?"

So Jarrod hadn't yet told her it was a lie! She

wondered why that was. No doubt he had his reasons, he had one for everything he did, unless of course Selina Howard did know it was a lie and they were continuing with this pretense to cover up their affair. That seemed the most likely explanation.

"We're still discussing it with my mother," Jarrod put in smoothly. "She insists it can't be arranged in a few weeks."

"I've never met your mother." Selina put her hand through the crook of his arm. "Introduce me."

"Excuse us," Jarrod said politely, leading the beautiful blond woman over to where his mother was chatting quite easily with some of Jarrod's employees.

Brooke looked at Charles Howard nervously, returning his smile. "I believe you've been away on business," she said conversationally, feeling extraordinarily shy in the company of this well-known man.

He nodded. "For over a week now. I returned at seven o'clock this evening."

"Then I'm very honored that you've come straight to my birthday party."

"I had to see the girl who has managed to capture the elusive Jarrod. I thought he was a confirmed bachelor. I can see why he changed his mind."

She blushed at his intended compliment, looking up sharply as she heard Selina Howard's throaty chuckle. The two of them had left Jarrod's mother now and were standing to one side of the room deep in conversation.

Charles followed her gaze, frowning as he saw his wife's hand on Jarrod's arm. He looked back at Brooke. "You'll have to forgive Selina," he said gently. "She's never been able to accept the fact that she's a married woman."

"Sorry?" she pretended ignorance, all the time aware of just how close Jarrod and this man's wife were standing.

Charles sighed. "My wife likes to flirt. But she doesn't mean anything by it," he added hastily. "At least, not usually," he muttered, watching his wife through narrowed eyes.

For such a successful businessman, Charles Howard certainly didn't understand his wife as he should, although he obviously had suspicions about her relationship with Jarrod. That wasn't surprising in the circumstances, Brooke felt as if everyone could see that possessive hand on *her* fiancé's arm.

She felt relieved when the small band at one end of the room began to play, moving into Charles Howard's arms at his request that they dance together. He was an amusing companion, very attractive, but nevertheless she still knew the exact moment when Jarrod stepped onto the dance floor with the beautiful Selina. And she resented the way the woman's arms were clasped around his neck, her body molded to him as she moved to the music. They made no attempt to dance in the conventional way and she knew Charles Howard had noticed them, too.

Jarrod's father claimed her for the next dance, and she felt the tension start to leave her body. If Jarrod had hoped to cover his affair with the other woman by keeping up this phony engagement he needn't have bothered. Charles Howard was very, very suspicious of his wife's friendship with him now and it would take drastic measures to allay those suspicions.

And the fact that Jarrod had now danced with the woman three times in succession would not help the situation. Brooke was keeping her eyes on Charles Howard and knew that he was aware of his wife's every move.

"Jarrod really surprised you this evening, didn't he," Clifford Stone remarked with a grin. "Springing this party on you."

She smiled up at him as they danced. "He certainly did," she agreed.

"Has he given you his gift, yet?"

"He gave me this gown. And I would like to thank

you once again for the lovely pearl necklace you gave
me. It's very beautiful.'' And something she had told
Jarrod she couldn't accept. He had cuttingly told her
she would do as she was told. Perhaps for the moment
she would, but later she would see it returned.

"We're just glad you like it; Sarah assured me that
the modern setting of the necklace was perfectly suitable. And although it's a charming gown I'm sure I
can tell you without spoiling any of Jarrod's fun that it
isn't your birthday gift from him. That's something
very special."

Like any other woman when told something like this
she now felt a burning curiosity to know what the gift
could be. Unless Jarrod had just told his parents this so
that they should think a lot of thought had gone into his
present to her. Not that she wanted anything else from
him, he had given her far too much already, including
this huge ring glittering on her finger like a brand of
possession.

Dave claimed her for a dance next, looking very
handsome in black trousers and a white evening jacket.
He wasted no time in coming straight to what was on his
mind. "What's my big brother doing with the blond
bombshell?"

Brooke was startled by his straightforwardness, but
she should have expected it after Sunday—Dave
wasn't one to mince his words. She arched one eyebrow. "Do you mean Mrs. Howard?" she asked innocently.

"So that's who she is! Yes, what's Jarrod doing
with the lovely Selina?"

She looked over his shoulder at the other couple.
"Dancing, I would say."

His hold tightened as he pulled her closer into his
arms. "I know that," he said in disgust. "But she's a
bit...well, she clings a bit. And she's monopolizing
Jarrod's attention, she had been for the last half hour
or so."

"It could be the other way around, you know."

He frowned. "What do you mean?"

"I mean Jarrod could be monopolizing her," she pointed out wryly.

Dave looked down at her. "When he's just got engaged to you? I don't believe it."

Brooke gave a hollow laugh. "Being engaged to someone doesn't mean you suddenly stop noticing how attractive other people are."

"Does that mean you could come to like me?" he asked softly against her earlobe.

"Dave!" she looked shocked. "I'm engaged to your brother."

"Do you love him?"

"Very much," she nodded.

He sighed. "Lucky Jarrod. I wonder if you would have fallen for me if we'd met first. I'd like to think so."

She had known that he liked her by his attitude toward her over the weekend, but she hadn't imagined it had been this much. "I would, too," she said gently. "But I'm afraid that as soon as I saw Jarrod I knew he was the one for me. It was just something I instinctively knew."

"Well, I instinctively think we should break up his little scene with the lovely Mrs. Howard. That woman means trouble if you don't watch her."

If only he knew! Selina Howard had been the cause of all her trouble of late. "So how do you expect me to get Jarrod away from her?"

He took hold of her hand and began to make his way through the other dancers. "Just leave it to me," he turned around to murmur. "I'll get her off your back."

Once he reached the other couple he tapped his brother on the shoulder, grinning in the face of Jarrod's obvious displeasure. He smiled at Selina Howard. "I'm Jarrod's brother, Mrs. Howard," he introduced him-

Could <u>you</u> dare love a man like this?

YES, eavesdrop on Leon and Helen in the searing pages of "Gates of Steel" by the celebrated best-selling romance author, Anne Hampson. She has crafted a story of passion and daring that will hold you in its spell until the final word is read.

You'll meet Leon, Helen and others, because they all live in the exciting world of *Harlequin Presents,* and all four books shown here are your FREE GIFTS to introduce you to the monthly home subscription plan of *Harlequin Presents.*

A Home Subscription

It's the easiest and most convenient way to get every one of the exciting *Harlequin Presents* novels! And now, with a home subscription plan you won't miss *any* of these true-to-life stories, and you don't even have to go out looking for them. You pay nothing extra for this convenience, there are no additional charges...you don't even pay for postage! Fill out and send us the handy coupon now, and we'll send you 4 exciting *Harlequin Presents* novels absolutely FREE!

Mail this coupon today!

Harlequin Presents...

Get your
Harlequin Presents
Home Subscription NOW!

▶ For exciting
details, see special
offer inside.

- ● Never miss a title!
- ● Get them first—straight from the presses!
- ● No additional costs for home delivery!
- ● These first 4 novels are yours FREE!

**Business
Reply Mail**

No Postage Stamp
Necessary if Mailed
in Canada

Postage will be paid by

**Harlequin Reader Service
Stratford (Ontario)
N5A 6W2**

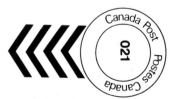

self. "And I've been longing to meet you all evening. Would you give me this dance?"

She couldn't do much else in the circumstances and Brooke tried to pretend she hadn't seen the wink Dave gave her over the other woman's shoulder as he whisked her away. She looked uncertainly at Jarrod as he towered over her.

"Did Dave think that up on his own or did you put him up to it?" he rasped.

"I don't know what you mean," she evaded.

"I'm pretty damn sure my little brother had no intention of going near Selina before he had that last dance with you." His look was grim. "You must have given him the idea."

Her eyes snapped, deeply violet in color. "It wouldn't occur to you that people have begun to gossip about the time you're spending with your mistress, that your own brother wanted to know exactly what was going on. Oh, no, you wouldn't think about that, would you. Because that's just what happened, so don't blame me for the fool you're making of yourself."

Jarrod pulled her roughly into his arms, moving angrily to the slow melodious music. "Okay, point taken. But don't talk to me like that again."

"Someone has to tell you," she said heatedly, stiff and unrelaxed in his arms. "And I think I should also tell you that we might as well forget about this phony engagement. You aren't fooling anyone, especially Charles Howard. He knows exactly what's going on between you and his wife."

His gray eyes narrowed. "Did he tell you that?" he demanded.

"He's been watching you all evening, and there's been plenty to see. If you can't keep your hands off her then you shouldn't have invited her here."

"I have a better idea." He pulled her so close to him she could feel the taut outline of his body. "If we're seen to be so much in love that we seem inseparable people will forget I was ever with Selina tonight."

"I wouldn't count on her husband forgetting."

Jarrod put her arms around his shoulders. "He will if you give a good performance."

"A good performance?"

"Act as if you love me," he explained roughly.

But she did! "Why should I do that? That would prove nothing, except that I'm in love with a man who loves another woman. I'm not going to make myself appear any more ridiculous than I do already."

His gray eyes bore down into hers. "You'll do this, Brooke, or you'll learn just what humiliation really is," he told her grimly.

She flinched at the look in his eyes. "Meaning?"

"Meaning that if you found my talking to Selina embarrassing you'll find I can do much worse things than that. I could make things so bad for you you'll feel like dying of shame. Especially as my family already consider us to be lovers," he added cruelly.

Brooke gasped. "They don't! Your mother said—"

"My mother believed me about the weekend. I said nothing about us not sleeping together at other times. I'm thirty-seven, Brooke, I haven't lived that long without a certain amount of physical relationships. I admit it, I'm not ashamed of the fact. So as my fiancée they would naturally expect us to be... well, I'm sure you can draw your own conclusions."

"Oh, God!" She danced against him automatically, uncaring that they were moving slowly to music that required much faster movements. They looked like a couple so much in love that they wanted only to be close to each other, everything else irrelevant to both of them.

If only that were the case, but she wasn't even aware of the music or the other people in the room. She hadn't thought of people assuming they had that sort of relationship, and she now found it so embarrassing she couldn't look anywhere but at him.

"That's terrible," she groaned.

Jarrod laughed, a deep throaty sound that mocked. "Don't be such an innocent, Brooke. Engaged couples often do, you know."

"So you keep saying. But it isn't my idea of an engagement," she said resentfully.

"You're nothing but a little prude."

"At least I have some morals," she burst out angrily. "Unlike some people. Doesn't it bother you that Charles Howard is a friend of yours, that people openly know of your affair with his wife?"

He had that cold angry look on his face now. "Would you believe me if I said it did?"

"No."

"That's what I thought, and that's why I've made no effort to deny your accusations. You've already made up your mind about me and I wouldn't like to ruin any of your illusions."

"I doubt you could ever do that," she scorned. "Everyone warned me when I came to work for you, everyone knew your reputation with women. But I still thought you—"

"Yes?" he prompted.

She hesitated about continuing, realizing she had been about to admit to her attraction to him. "You're very attractive," she finished abruptly. "I'm sure I'm not the first female to tell you that. I thought you quite romantic, very sophisticated. But then I found I didn't like the games sophisticated people play, that I didn't like *you* very much. I like you even less now."

He looked down at her as her bright head rested on his shoulder. "No one would believe it to look at you," he taunted.

Instantly she moved away from him, but he stilled her movements, making her gasp at the force of his body on hers. "Let me go!" she ordered. "Stop making an exhibition out of us."

He forced her to remain still. "You're doing that," he growled angrily. "People expect to see us gazing into each other's eyes, so do it!"

She obstinately continued to look away from him. "I don't like your eyes," she declared childishly. "They're cruel and unkind." And incredibly sexy, she could have added. Gray eyes that could be coolly calculating and could also be dark with sleepy passion, passion she had aroused only once but assuredly knew existed.

"They probably are at this moment," he agreed carelessly.

"They are most of the time," she added bitchily.

He laughed at her anger. "Okay, off you go and act the gracious hostess." He pushed her away from him. "Your acting is lousy—I'll have to give you some private lessons."

Her face aflame she rushed away from the taunting mockery of his face, well aware of what sort of lessons he had in mind. And she had no defense against the brand of seduction he practiced.

She found herself standing with Jean, her boyfriend Nathanial off dancing with one of the other girls from the Stone office building. "Everything all right?" she asked her friend.

Jean gave her a glowing smile. "Lovely. Mr. Stone's family are all very nice. I've had a chat with all of them and they aren't in the least snobbish. His father is a real charmer."

"Yes. Thank you for the perfume, Jean. It's my favorite brand."

"That's what I thought. This actually seems real now, your engagement and everything. It seemed unbelievable at first, but now I've seen the two of you together I can understand how you feel. I was so excited yesterday when Mr. Stone invited Nathanial and me to your party."

"I knew absolutely nothing about it," Brooke smiled. "Jarrod's very good at keeping secrets." He was also a better actor than she was if Jean genuinely believed him to be in love with her.

"Mmm, I could see how disappointed you were today when everyone seemed to have forgotten your birthday. As if we could!"

"Jarrod explained how you were sworn to secrecy." She was once again aware that Jarrod was talking to Selina Howard.

She chatted to Jean and her other friends for the next hour or more and never once did Jarrod leave his mistress's side. Brooke found this very humiliating and she knew Charles Howard was displeased by it, too.

She felt quite relieved when the party eventually broke up and Jarrod drove her home. She had more or less decided to give him back his ring by the time they reached her home. She could put up with this deceit, but she wouldn't be humiliated in this way.

She got out of the car as he held the door open for her. "Thank you for my party," she said formally. "It was very thoughtful of you."

He quirked an eyebrow. "It was all I could do on your twenty-first birthday. It would have looked very strange if I hadn't given you a party."

Brooke bridled angrily. "I didn't think you had made the gesture out of kindness."

"I'm sure you know me better than to think that," he taunted.

"I'm getting to know you very well," she snapped. "And what I'm learning I don't like." She turned on her heel to enter the building.

"Aren't you going to invite me in for coffee?" he called after her softly.

She turned around fiercely to look at him, subconsciously noticing how handsome he looked as he leaned back against the sleek car they had driven up in only seconds earlier. "Do you want to come in for coffee?" she asked breathlessly.

"Would I be asking if I didn't? Besides, someone has to carry in your presents."

She shrugged. "Okay, then, you had better come in." She went in without bothering to wait and see if he followed her.

Once inside she put her jacket and handbag in the bedroom before walking over to the kitchen to prepare the requested coffee. She was only halfway across the lounge when a hand shot out and pulled her hard against an unyielding body.

She looked up at Jarrod with defiant eyes. "What do you want now? Haven't I already made recompense enough for one evening?"

Gray eyes glittered down at her before the dark head swooped down and firm punishing lips descended on hers, forcing her soft lips apart with ruthless brutality. For long seconds the world seemed to spin dizzily as she clung to him for support. And then she was free, rubbing her hand across her bruised mouth as he moved away from her.

Her eyes were pools of deep violet hurt as she gazed up at him reproachfully. "What did you do that for?" she asked accusingly.

He looked unperturbed, a devilish glint in his gray eyes. "You've been asking for that all evening."

"I have not! I—"

"Oh, yes, you have," he told her calmly, unmoved by her anger. "You've been giving me filthy looks all night and—"

"Only because of the time you spent with that woman! Everyone noticed it and—"

"And launching into a string of accusations every time we've spoken," he continued as if she hadn't interrupted him. "You've just received your punishment, remember it for future reference. I have my own method of revenge. And just for the record, I couldn't give a damn about what other people think. Now—" he flexed his shoulder muscles "—perhaps you wouldn't mind driving me home? Forget the coffee, that was just a way of getting in here."

Brooke frowned. "Drive you home? Don't you feel well?"

"I feel fine." He handed her the car keys. "But as it's your car I thought perhaps you might like to park it downstairs. Besides, I'd like to be with you the first time you drive it—an Aston Martin is slightly different to a Mini," he added mockingly.

She paled. "That car...the Aston Martin...it's *mine*?" She looked down at the car keys in disbelief.

He nodded. "Your birthday present from me. Of course, if you would rather have something else, a Porsche or a Ferrari, then I don't mind changing it."

She gave a choked laugh. Jarrod had given her an Aston Martin for her birthday and said she could change it if she preferred another car. Change it! It was a dream of a car—and Jarrod had *given* it to her!

CHAPTER SIX

SHE SHOOK her head. "You can't mean it," she said huskily.

He shrugged. "Of course I mean it. It should be quite easy to change the make of car, and the color, too, if you would prefer something different."

She gave a breathless laugh. "That wasn't what I meant. I meant that you can't really want to give me a car like that for my birthday. I don't expect anything from you."

He frowned darkly, all humor leaving his face. "I didn't get you it because it was expected of me," he rasped coldly. "Every girl should have something special for her twenty-first birthday."

"But a car like that!" she pointed out desperately.

"I'm glad you like it."

"I love it, but I couldn't possibly—"

"My wife will be expected to have a style of car fitting for her position in life."

Brooke gasped. "Your wife! But I'm not going to be your wife. This is all an act, a ruse."

He nodded agreement, sitting down in one of her armchairs. "You might as well sit down, too. I think we have some talking to do."

She dropped into the chair rather than sat down. "We...we do?"

"Yes." He watched her through narrowed thoughtful gray eyes. "Now don't start to panic when you hear what I'm going to say. All right?"

"All right," she agreed apprehensively.

"Okay, then," he sighed. "I think we should get married."

"What!" She sprang up out of the chair to glare down at him as he watched her so calmly. He had no right to look so composed when she had been reduced to a quivering mass of nerves! "What did you say?" she asked shakily.

"You said you wouldn't panic," he reminded her impatiently. "And if that isn't panic you're showing, it's a very good impression of it."

Brooke gave him a disgusted look. "Of course it's panic. When I said I wouldn't I had no idea you were going to say something so outrageous."

"It wasn't outrageous, I merely suggested that we do what everyone is expecting of us and get married. What's so outrageous about that?"

She almost choked in her effort to give him all the reasons in one go, finally saying the one that seemed to matter the most. "We aren't in love with each other."

Jarrod raised one dark eyebrow. "Does that matter?"

"I would have thought so if we intended getting married."

"It's not necessary. We have something else equally as volatile."

Her eyes widened. "We do?"

Instantly his eyes darkened almost to black and he stood up in one slow fluid movement. Brooke stood mesmerized as he came toward her, her head back to look up at him as his arms passed around her waist to pull her close against the lean length of his body.

"Wh—what do we have?" She fought for sanity, aware of the weakness of her lower limbs at his closeness, of the even rise and fall of his chest just inches in front of her fixed gaze.

"Don't you know?" he murmured, his dark head bending so he could nuzzle his mouth against her arched throat.

Slow drugging kisses to her skin had her breathless within seconds, her arms clinging around his neck, her pulse sounding so loud it seemed like a bass drum to her ears.

She cleared her throat. "No, I...I don't know."

His strong firm hands ran experimentally over her body, lingering on her taut breasts. "Oh, you know, Brooke," he groaned throatily. "Your body knows it, too."

His mouth claimed hers, her lips blossoming beneath the cajoling seduction he chose to exert, knowing with all his experience that he could arouse her to the heights so easily. She gave up all pretense of appearing unmoved, knowing that she gave herself away at a touch of those sure, tanned hands.

Her breath was coming in short gasps when his lips finally released hers, her eyes glazed with feeling. She shivered as his mouth traveled across her cheek to her earlobe, his hands molding the contours of her body to the hardness of his.

"Jarrod?" she queried tremulously.

He didn't raise his head. "Can't you feel it, too, the attraction between us?"

She knew she was attracted to him, she couldn't deny it when she melted in his arms like this, but how did he feel about her? He wasn't a man to show his feelings for any woman, except the beautiful Mrs. Howard, and Brooke knew she was no competition for her.

She moved against his probing mouth, cherishing these few moments in his arms. These kisses were nothing like his earlier punishing onslaught, and she was loving every moment of being this close to him.

"Don't you feel it?" he persisted, straightening slightly to look down at her, his eyes black with desire.

"Yes, I...I suppose I do." She was embarrassed by the look in his eyes. "But what difference does that make? You're in love with Selina Howard."

He scowled. "Forget Selina for God's sake! I'm only interested in you and me at this moment in time."

"Forget her!" Brooke scoffed. "How can I forget the woman you're openly having an affair with?"

His hands tightened painfully on her arms. "You're going to accuse me of that just once too often," he ground out viciously. "But I want you, Brooke, and I don't think you'll let me have you any other way but through marriage."

"You're right."

"Okay, so we get married."

Her head was thrown back defiantly. "I may only be a little nobody but I wouldn't marry a man knowing he was in love with someone else."

"You'll marry me," he promised. "I'll see to that."

His head lowered and his kiss was totally savage, a deliberate onslaught on the senses, and in her already heightened state she had no way of denying him her full response. She shivered in sensuous delight as he slipped her gown off one shoulder to caress her skin with his rousing lips.

Jarrod swung her effortlessly up into his arms, his lips still firmly in control of her as she made to protest at his progress toward her bedroom. But those lips just kept on kissing her until she felt drugged by her own emotions, making not a murmur of protest as he lowered her down onto the bed before joining her with such rapidity his lips never left hers.

Her gown was no barrier to his searching hands and her breasts flowered under his touch as he slipped the gown completely off her shoulders and down her body. He discarded his jacket, removing his bow tie, and leaving it to her to do the rest.

Brooke needed no second bidding, completely unbuttoning the silky shirt to slip it off his shoulders. It wasn't the first time she had seen his naked torso and yet the heat of his body against her own bare skin was enough to launch her into ecstatic delight.

"Do you want me now?" he asked as his lips teased the tip of one taut breast.

"I..." she gasped with the pleasure of feeling he was evoking. "Oh, God, Jarrod! Please stop now, I can't stand any more."

"Do you want me?" he repeated harshly.

She flung her head from side to side in an effort to escape those pleasure-giving but drugging lips. "Don't make me say it, Jarrod," she begged. "Don't make me answer."

He pinned her to the bed by her wrists, his legs also helping to hold her immovable. "Tell me you want me, Brooke. Tell me!"

"I want you, I want you!" she cried, her eyes wild.

"And you'll marry me?" His hold on her wrists tightened, forcing her to answer him.

"No, I—"

His lips descended before she had time to even think of evasive action. The kisses he devoured her with over the next few minutes were just as destructive as his earlier caresses, and Brooke's hands were buried deep in the dark thickness of his hair long before he raised his head again.

His breathing was ragged and his heartbeat sounded just as loud as her own. "If you're very wise, Brooke, you'll agree to marry me. It could just be the one thing that will stop me taking you here and now."

She knew he meant what he said and she also knew she wouldn't be able to resist him; he had aroused her too easily for her to be able to do that. At least he was offering her marriage, even while knowing it wasn't necessary. He was a man of experience and he would undoubtedly know he could take her any time he chose, without the least opposition from her.

But still she fought against the fate of having to marry a man in love with another woman and feeling only desire for the woman he offered marriage to. He may think that second best was better than nothing, but she had other ideas. "I can't do it, it wouldn't be right."

"Right!" he scorned. "What's *right* about desire? It's a gnawing ache inside you that has to be assuaged. I want you and I'm not prepared to see my brother walk off with the prize."

She struggled against him in the darkness but all her efforts were futile against his superior strength. "What does Dave have to do with us?" she demanded, admitting her defeat by slumping back against the pillows.

He gave a harsh laugh. "My little brother is already half in love with you—and don't deny it because you know it's true. And he would offer you marriage. But I don't aim to let him have you. You're already half mine and I mean to possess all of you."

"I am not yours!" she exploded angrily. "I belong to whom I want to belong," she added defiantly.

His gray eyes glittered down at her dangerously. "And who else have you already belonged to?" His eyes slid insolently over her almost naked body. "No doubt you've used the power of this delectable body to taunt the hell out of other men."

This time she did wrench away from him and up off the bed altogether, tugging her gown back over her shoulders and pulling up the zipper with agitated fingers. She turned to glare at him, resenting the easy way he sat up on the bed and began to pull on his hastily discarded shirt.

"What I have or haven't done in my lifetime is none of your affair," she pushed back her tousled hair. "Get out of here. Right now."

He stood up slowly, buttoning his shirt before tucking it back into the low waistband of his trousers. He watched her through amused eyes as she threw his tie at him.

"Get out of here, damn you!" she almost screamed the words.

He slipped on his jacket in unhurried movements, putting the bow tie in his pocket. "I'll bring you to your knees before I've finished with you," he taunted softly, "I'll have you begging me to marry you, you'll see."

"Like hell you will!" she blazed.

"Oh, I will, Brooke. I'll twist you up in knots so tight you'll be glad to marry me just to find the release I can give you."

"Physical gratification," she said in disgust.

"Don't mock it," he warned. "You won't find it so disgusting in a couple of weeks, either." He smiled, a cruel taunting smile. "I'll look forward to seeing you grovel."

"Go to hell!"

"I'm going home," he corrected mockingly. "But I'll see you tomorrow evening."

She looked at him sharply. "Tomorrow evening?"

"Mmm," he nodded. "The start of the torture."

She shook her head dazedly. "I don't understand you. Why me?" she pleaded.

"Why not you? I want you, not just once or twice, but for all time. I could take you now but if I did that you would never want to see me again. So I'm going to marry you."

"But what of Selina Howard?"

He shrugged. "I can't marry her, she already has a very possessive husband."

"Oh, I see, you mean to marry me because you can't marry the woman you really want."

He gave a throaty chuckle. "You silly child," he scolded almost gently. "You felt my desire for you a moment ago, that was for you—no one else." He bent his head to claim her lips in a brief kiss. "Tomorrow I begin my pursuit in earnest. I hope you're ready for that."

"Oh, go away!" she retorted, more shaken by his threat than she cared to admit.

She waited until she heard the door close behind him before breaking down, deep wracking sobs shuddering through her body. He had no right to play on her desire in this way, no right to torment her as he had. And if he meant to do what he said it could only get worse.

"It was a fantastic party last night," Jean enthused halfway through the morning, the first break the two of them had had in their daily routine.

"Thank you," Brooke replied distantly, unwilling to enter into any conversation about last night. She was doing her best to forget the events of the latter part of the evening and hoped Jarrod had done the same.

"Everyone said what a great time they had." Jean obviously hadn't noticed her reluctance concerning the subject.

"Jarrod seems to be adept at arranging things like that."

"Your Jarrod's dreamy," Jean became starry-eyed. "I never would have thought him capable of being that human. He always appeared haughty and slightly removed from the rest of us poor mortals."

He was also devious and selfish and totally without morals. He used people, well he used her, shamelessly. And he was going to get even more demanding. She had to admit that the thought of it both excited and frightened her. And she wasn't sure which feeling was going to be predominant next time she saw him.

"He's just a man." She shrugged. "Like any other he needs a woman." Often in the plural, she could have added. He would obviously still be seeing Mrs. Howard even while determined to make Brooke want to marry him.

Jean raised a questioning eyebrow. "You sound very...well, a bit fed up actually. Aren't you really excited about marrying Mr. Stone, I know I would be.''

She wouldn't be marrying him if she had her way—no matter how much she really wanted to. With his experience of women he would soon realize that she was in love with him, probably believing that she would be gullible enough to put up with his affairs. Well, she wouldn't marry him and give him that power over her, and she wouldn't become his wife to hide his affair with another woman, either.

She smiled wanly. "Sorry, Jean. Late nights don't agree with me.''

Jean grimaced. "Me neither. But it was such a lovely surprise for you. Mr. Stone was—''

She broke off and turning in the direction of her gaze Brooke saw the reason why. Jarrod had just stepped out of his private elevator and was walking with purposeful strides over to the reception desk.

Brooke blushed under the force of his unflinching stare, unconsciously noting how attractive he looked in his dark business suit. She fidgeted nervously as she waited for him to reach her desk, looking impatiently at the diamond ring he forced her to wear as proof of his possession.

As if he had seen that look he deliberately lifted up the hand containing his ring, his eyes glittering with barely suppressed humor as he watched her reaction. She steeled herself to make none and saw his amusement deepen. His manner gave her the feeling of a very small mouse being tormented by a cruel feline.

"Brooke, darling," he murmured softly, his hold on her hand not loosening. "I'm going to be out the rest of the day.''

She wanted to ask what that had to do with her but knew he wouldn't let her get away with that. "Yes?'' she queried huskily, all the time conscious of his thumb slowly caressing the palm of her hand.

"So I brought your car in today—as you were too tired to drive me home last night," he added mockingly. "And I'll be using it to go to my business appointment." His mouth tightened as he saw the disbelieving look in her eyes that it was a business meeting and her hand was instantly set free. "I just want to reassure you that I'll be around at eight-thirty and you can have your car back then."

"Thank you." She didn't want his damned car! And she didn't want to see him tonight, either—didn't want him to destroy her peace of mind any more than he already had.

He bent forward and kissed her lingeringly on her parted lips. It wasn't a caress he hurried over, and by the time he raised his head Brooke was breathless—with embarrassment *and* excitement.

She fumed up at him silently, her eyes deep violet pools of frustrated anger. How dare he! How dare he kiss her here in full view of anyone who cared to look. And plenty of people were doing just that!

"Just to keep me going until tonight, darling," he murmured throatily, taunting her with the steely glint in his eyes. He straightened, turning to smile at the gaping Jean. "Good morning," he grinned at her. "No ill effects from last night, I hope?"

Jean glowed. "No, thank you, Mr. Stone. I had a lovely time."

"Good." He nodded to them both. "Goodbye for now then, ladies. I'll see you later, Brooke," he added with a warmth that almost made her cringe.

She didn't answer him, pretending an interest in the person making inquiries at her desk. The poor man had to repeat himself three times before she heard what he was trying to ask her. She finally sent him off quite happily to the fifth floor.

She hardly dared turn and look at Jean once they were restored to peace and quiet again, but she knew that inevitably she had to. She sighed. "Okay, Jean, you're right, he *is* very attractive. But he...well, he unnerves me, especially here at work."

Jean grinned. "He would unnerve me, too, if he kissed me likc that."

Brooke blushed anew. "Don't tease, Jean. I'm embarrassed enough already."

This time her friend took the hint and changed the subject, talking about things that were much less personal to Brooke.

By eight-fifteen that evening she had worked herself up into a great state of nerves. His display in reception today had more than shown her that he meant to carry out his threat to make her want him enough to marry him.

But she already did! She wanted him now, he had no need to make her want him any more. How was she supposed to cope with the brand of sensual attraction he exuded with every pore of his body. She had the feeling she wasn't going to be able to—and he knew it.

Jarrod arrived at exactly eight-thirty, walking into her apartment before holding out the car keys to her. "Yours," he said with a grin.

Brooke weighed the keys in her hand. "I would rather not if you don't mind."

He ignored her words, settling himself comfortably on the sofa. He was dressed more casually than she had ever seen him before and this casualness gave their relationship an intimacy she had been determined to avoid. He wore tan leather boots, cream corduroy trousers that molded to the firm length of his thighs, a cream silk shirt opened almost down to his waist, and a short brown leather jerkin. He looked very tall and very attractive and her pulse raced just at the sight of him.

She looked down at her own clothes, realizing that her deliberate donning of denims and checked shirt had all been in vain. And she had the feeling that Jarrod had known exactly what she had been going to do, hence his own attire.

"Have you had dinner?" he asked.

"Yes, thank you. I don't want it, Jarrod," she said firmly, unconsciously using his first name.

"I've already eaten, too."

"Jarrod!" she glared at him. "You're deliberately ignoring me."

Gray eyes raked over her with slow appraisal and she was blushing profusely by the time his gaze settled back on her face. "I'm not ignoring you, Brooke," he denied huskily. "The opposite I would have thought."

"You know what I mean," she sighed. "I don't want the car. It... it smacks too much like payment," she said defiantly.

"Payment for what?" he asked softly.

"For... for... I don't know what for!" She gave him a furious look. "Yes I do! It looks like payment for services rendered."

He gave a throaty chuckle, not angered as she had expected him to be, *hoped* he would be. If she angered him enough there was always the chance he might walk out. But there didn't appear to be much anger about him as he smiled up at her, sitting forward to remove his jacket.

He turned back the cuffs of his shirt to just below his elbows. "It's very hot tonight," he offered by way of explanation. "And I haven't noticed you providing much of a service," he added tauntingly.

Brooke's cheeks flamed fiery red, the situation, as always, backfiring on her. "Perhaps you like to pay in advance," she returned bitchily.

"Not usually," he replied thoughtfully. "You could get let down that way. You know, a case of take the money and run."

"Then take back your damned car!"

"It isn't mine. It was bought in your name and is registered to you."

She turned away. "You don't understand—or you don't want to. I'm an ordinary working girl, okay I accept that for the moment I'm involved in your life, but when that's over I'm not even going to be able to afford the insurance on the car let alone the weekly gas."

"It's never going to be over between us, Brooke. You're mine and before long you're going to admit it to me."

"On bended knees," she scorned.

He nodded. "If necessary."

"Never!"

Jarrod gave a knowing smile. "Never is a long long time, Brooke, darling. And I can be quite determined when I make up my mind to do something. Ask any of my business colleagues."

"Oh, I don't need to do that, I already know how domineering you can be."

"Then why don't you sit down and relax?" he invited huskily, patting the sofa beside him.

Brooke moved away jerkily. "Why don't you go and see Selina Howard? I'm sure she would be overjoyed to see you."

"I doubt it," he said dryly. "She and Charles always spend their wedding anniversary together, I wouldn't like to interrupt."

"Oh."

He was openly laughing at her now. "Sit down, Brooke," he repeated. "No, not over there," he said as she went to sit in one of the armchairs. "Over here, next to me."

"No, thank you," she answered primly. "What are you planning to do this evening?"

"Nothing, absolutely nothing." He leaned back against the sofa, legs splayed out in front of him. "Why, what did you have in mind?"

"Nothing. But . . . but surely you don't intend to just spend the evening here with me?"

"And the night, too, if you would let me."

"I won't!"

"I didn't think so. Put some music on, hmm?"

She moved to the record cabinet. "What sort of music do you like?"

"Something romantic," he murmured.

"R-romantic?"

"Mmm," he said throatily. "Then you can come and sit next to me and I'll whisper sweet nothings in your shell-like ear."

She gave him a furious look for his mockery, deliberately choosing one of Leo Sayer's L.P.'s that was anything but romantic. She sat down with a smile of satisfaction, enjoying the music but knowing it didn't meet Jarrod's approval.

When it moved on to the second number Jarrod stood up and turned the record off. "Not that I don't like Leo Sayer, but those sort of songs don't exactly stir the senses."

"They weren't meant to," she said determinedly.

"That's what I thought." He flicked through the extensive record collection, music of all kinds being her weakness. "Barry Manilow or Johnny Mathis?"

"Johnny Mathis, please," she answered instantly. "Some of Barry Manilow's tend to be a little sad."

Instead of going back to the sofa after putting on the requested record he came to sit on the arm of her chair. "We have a lot of the same tastes in music," he murmured softly.

Brooke obstinately looked away from him, although she could see his muscular thigh out of the corner of her eyes. "That's about all we do have in common," she told him curtly, determined not to be moved by his closeness.

But how could she not be when just to look at him aroused her! He was so handsome, so dynamic. But she must remember that even though he expressed a wish to make love to her, would even go to the length

of marrying her to get what he wanted, that all the
time he was having an affair with a married woman,
an affair that wouldn't stop on the event of his own
marriage.

These thoughts hardened her resolve not to be af-
fected by his closeness, by the all-male smell of him.
God, it was so destructive just being near him like
this.

His hand moved to touch one of her hot cheeks,
the thumb moving caressingly over her soft creamy
skin. "I think we have more than that in common,"
he said softly, his gray eyes never leaving her averted
face. "And we could have more if you would just let it
happen. Have you always had these inhibitions?"

Her gaze swung angrily to his taunting face only to
look hurriedly away again at the warmth in his eyes.
He was seducing her with a look and she couldn't
stand it. Before he could stop her she had moved out
of the chair and stood a few feet away watching him
warily.

"I don't have inhibitions at all. You just...you
just—"

"Yes?" he relaxed back in the chair she had so re-
cently vacated.

"I don't want to have an affair!"

"Neither do I, not unless it's going to lead to marriage." He sighed. "Sit down again, Brooke. I promise
to stay right here. We'll talk, nothing else."

"What do we have to talk about?"

He shrugged. "You can tell me more about your
childhood. This aunt of yours, what was she like, besides her desire to hit out at a child."

Off the subject of marriage she relaxed slightly,
moving to the sofa to sit down. "She was a lot older
than my mother, there was a fifteen-year difference in
their ages."

."And this aunt never married?"

"No, but then I could have been partly responsible

for that. Having a five-year-old child to look after would daunt a lot of men."

Jarrod shook his head. "Your aunt would already have been fortyish when she took you into her care, plenty of time to marry if she had wanted to."

"No, you see she had to look after my mother for several years, too."

"Ah, I see."

"Do you have to say it like that?" she asked resentfully.

He raised his eyebrows. "Sorry. It just seemed to me—"

"I'm well aware of what it seemed to you. But Aunt Emma always said she didn't want to marry."

"She didn't like men," he stated dryly.

"Not my father, anyway."

His eyes quickened with interest. "Are you sure? How old was your father when he died?"

"He was ten years older than my mother so that would make him thirty-five." Her brow creased in puzzlement. "What are you implying?"

"Only that the emotion your aunt felt toward your father may not have been dislike."

"You're surely not trying to say that Aunt Emma *fancied* my father?" Her horror was evident in her face.

"Is that so hard to believe?"

"It's disgusting!"

"What's so disgusting about a healthy woman feeling attracted to a handsome man?"

"But the man was my father and he was married to Aunt Emma's *sister*."

He shrugged. "That doesn't mean she couldn't fall in love with him."

Brooke stood up to pace the room. "I can't believe it— She couldn't— But it...." He was right! She knew with startling clarity that he had guessed the reason for her aunt's hatred and jealousy of her sister's happiness. All these years she had wondered at her aunt's resentment of her and within a few days of knowing her Jarrod had discovered that reason.

"I'm right, aren't I?" he asked gently.

"Yes," she choked. "I think you are."

He moved quickly on seeing her distress, sitting down beside her on the sofa and pulling her into his arms. "Hey," he crooned softly into her hair. "I didn't mean to upset you."

"It was...was just such a shock," she mumbled against his chest. "I didn't mean to be emotional about it."

"I shouldn't have surprised you with it like that." He lifted her chin. "I could be wrong, you know."

"No, you aren't," she sniffed inelegantly. "I should have realized before. It just never occurred to me."

"You would have to have a devious mind like mine to think of it," he murmured softly, his mouth only inches away from her own. "Oh, Brooke, Brooke, kiss me...."

"Jarrod...." She kissed him as never before, clinging to him in complete abandonment. What did all the fighting and arguing matter when she could be in his arms like this?

He took her lips in slow drugging kisses that wracked her body into sensuous pleasure, lowering her back against the length of the sofa before lying at her side.

Their caresses became fevered and she raised not one word of protest as he unbuttoned her shirt with sure quick movements, pushing aside the thin material to bury his face in her creamy skin.

"God, Brooke," he groaned raggedly. "Don't you ever wear a bra?" His voice thickened with desire as he took the tip of one hardened nipple into his mouth, arousing her body to even greater heights.

Her sharp intake of breath precluded her answer for several long pleasurable seconds. "I, er, I find them a cumbersome article of clothing," she said finally.

He raised his dark head to look down at her partly naked body. "Well, it's a sure fact you're lovely enough not to need one." He caressed her with hands that seemed to burn where they touched. "God, you're beautiful! So beautiful I'm almost afraid to touch you."

Her arms moved up over his shoulders, her hands entwining in the dark thickness of his hair. "Don't be afraid, Jarrod," she invited. "I like your touch."

With a suddenness that took her completely by surprise he moved away from her to stand up, the passionate man of seconds earlier gone as if it had never been. Only the sight of her own nakedness remained to show her that it hadn't all been a dream. She fastened her shirt with shaking fingers.

"It's getting late," he said abruptly. "I have to leave. Don't bother to drive me home, I can get a taxi. I'll see you sometime tomorrow evening. Good night." He didn't look at her again but slammed out of the apartment.

CHAPTER SEVEN

EVERY EVENING seemed to end the same way, they would talk for a while, listen to a few records, and then she would somehow find herself in Jarrod's arms. Each night she promised herself that this time it would be different, that she wouldn't give in to the sensuous pressure of his mouth or the demand in his eyes, but each time she betrayed her resolve.

Jarrod controlled these interludes in a way that was totally infuriating. He knew exactly when she had almost lost control of her senses, knew when she would deny him nothing—and that was the time he always broke up their embrace.

Brooke knew that he purposefully used these frustrating tactics, that it was all part of his plan to bring her to her knees, and yet there was nothing she could do to stop it happening. As soon as he touched her she melted.

But tonight she knew things were going to be different as soon as she opened the door to him, knew it by the elegant dinner suit he wore. He hadn't said they were going out so she didn't think she was included in his dinner engagement. She was right.

"Sorry I'm a little late." He bent to kiss her fleetingly on the lips.

Brooke had become accustomed to these casual caresses by now, although they still excited her. "Is there anything wrong?" she indicated the suit.

"I have to leave almost immediately," he said with irritation. "Something turned up unexpectedly."

"Oh." She gave him a knowing look.

Jarrod looked at her sharply. "Don't you believe me?"

She shrugged. "Why shouldn't I?"

"Because you don't," he said with certainty. "And I don't have the time to stay here and argue with you. An important business colleague arrived from the States this afternoon. I have to entertain him."

"Oh, I see, a night out with the boys, hmm?"

"God, you can be so infuriating at times. But perhaps your attitude proves you can be jealous. A good sign," he added with satisfaction.

"I wouldn't count on it being jealousy," she told him coolly. Disappointment was a better word. Each evening she wondered if she would be strong enough to hold out against him and yet now that he was leaving after only a few short minutes she was disappointed. "Elation might be a better word," she lied.

"Elation, is it!" he said grimly, pulling her effortlessly into his arms and forcing her lips apart with no sign of gentleness at all. He was bent on punishing her and although she didn't want to respond there was nothing she could do to stop herself.

By the time he had finished the onslaught she lay limp in his arms, her lips swollen and aroused, her eyes slightly glassy. Jarrod pushed aside her top to kiss her breasts, his tongue arousing her even further and giving her intense pleasure.

He drew back to look at her, passion blazing as he saw the desire in her face. "Damn Clive and his business dinner!" he groaned throatily. "I'd much rather stay here with you." He touched her hardened nipple. "Much rather," he repeated with agonizing intensity.

"But you can't." It was almost a question.

"No, I can't." His eyes half closed as he continued to look at her. "Oh, God, I want you!"

She wanted him, too, but common sense was starting to return. He could just be trying to trick her into admitting defeat, as he had done in the past. And that was the one thing she wasn't going to do, not if it meant becoming the wife of a man in love with another woman.

She looked pointedly at her wristwatch. "It's getting late, you'll be late for your dinner engagement."

He, too, looked at the time. "You're right, I have to leave now. How the hell I'm supposed to think and talk of business when all I have on my mind is you is going to be quite interesting. I'll probably babble about what a beautiful body you have in the middle of an important discussion," he said self-disgustedly.

Brooke pouted. "You don't consider my body important?"

His eyes darkened. "At the moment I consider it the most important thing in the world," he admitted thickly.

"But you'll get over it," she taunted.

"You think so?" His mouth moved to caress her throat. "I'm not so sure."

"You seemed to get over it every other night, so why not tonight?"

He looked down at her, a mocking smile lighting his cynical features. "That rankles, doesn't it?"

So she had fallen into his trap after all! She moved stiffly out of his restraining arms. "Why should it?" she asked carelessly. "I believe men get over these little disappointments much easier than women."

His snort of laughter showed his scorn for such a statement. "You have just proved to me that you know little or nothing about the mechanism of men. We don't get over our disappointment at all. We may be able to dampen things down a little, but inevitably it flares up again. You don't hear of many rape cases being carried out by women."

"But it does happen."

"Oh, sure," he grinned. "But even so I don't believe it can be classed as rape. He may have been coerced into it in the beginning, but a man really has to be willing. I'm sure you know what I mean, you aren't that innocent."

"I know what you mean," she answered, her cheeks fiery red.

He laughed. "I see you do."

"Shouldn't you be leaving now?"

"Embarrassing you, am I?" he mocked.

"Not at all," Brooke said sharply. "But you did say you were in a hurry. I was just reminding you."

"After arousing me so much I don't want to leave you at all," he said derisively. "God, you're torture to be with!"

"Then leave!" She turned away from him.

"I intend to—but I'll be back tomorrow. We'll go out to dinner and then on to a nightclub. Sunday we can spend the day together."

"You seem to take it for granted that you can organize my free time for me," she snapped resentfully.

He lifted her left hand, looking down at the ring he had put on her finger. "*This* gives me that right."

She snatched her hand away. "I've told you before, it gives you no rights at all. Please go." She pushed her hair back from her face. "Please, Jarrod," she implored him, before she broke down and begged him to stay.

"I'm going—but not because I want to." He claimed one last kiss before moving swiftly to the door. "I would get an early night, we could be out quite late tomorrow evening."

"I'll go to bed when I damn well please!" she turned on him angrily.

"I thought you might." He closed the door softly behind him.

Oh, he was so infuriating, getting under her guard all the time. If only he weren't so attractive—and so expert when it came to lovemaking. But so he should be, he had had plenty of experience—too damned much!

Once again he had left leaving her quite unsatisfied, having aroused her and then left her apartment. Oh, this time he had expressed disappointment at their parting, too, but it didn't ease the ache deep inside her or the restless feeling that would take hours to leave her.

When the doorbell rang again fifteen minutes later she thought Jarrod must have changed his mind and come back. Her face elated she ran to the door. "Oh, Jarrod, I..." she broke off as she saw who her visitor was. "Dave," she said weakly.

He looked a little hurt by her obvious disappointment at his identity. "I'm afraid so," he shrugged. "Perhaps I called at an inconvenient time. You're obviously expecting Jarrod." He turned away.

"Oh, no, no, I'm not." She put out a hand to delay him. "Jarrod's already been and gone. He has a business engagement this evening. I just thought...well, I thought he may have forgotten something." She could hardly say she had hoped he had come back to make love to her!

Dave looked slightly relieved. "So you aren't expecting him back tonight?"

"No." She opened the door farther. "Would you like to come in?"

"If you wouldn't mind."

"No, I...I would be glad of the company. It's strange really, but even with so many people living in London it can still be the loneliest place in the world. I suppose it's because everyone has their own circle of friends and they rarely move out of that circle." She was aware that she was babbling nervously, but she didn't seem able to stop herself.

Dave looked around her sitting room appreciatively. "Nice apartment you have here. You should see mine," he grimaced. "It's like a cupboard with a bed in it."

"Oh, but surely—"

"I know what you're going to say," he interrupted. "But I don't accept help from my family. Oh, they give me the usual boxes of food parents seem to think their children who have left home need, but that's all. I simply wouldn't fit in at the hospital if I was living in the lap of luxury while all my friends lived on the poverty line."

"And is that important to you?"

"Fitting in?" He shrugged. "I suppose so. Do you mind if I sit down?"

She blushed at her lack of manners. "Please do. I'm sorry I didn't think of it earlier. The surprise of seeing you I suppose," she explained nervously. She sat down opposite him as he sat in one of the armchairs. "I wasn't expecting anyone else tonight."

"No, it is rather late." He looked at his wristwatch. "Nine-fifteen. Did Jarrod leave very long ago?"

"He's been gone about half an hour I would think."

Dave grinned. "It could have been rather embarrassing if he had been here. I know how suspicious my big brother can be," he said by way of explanation. "Lucky I picked a night when he had to be somewhere else."

Brooke would have said fortunate, not lucky. Jarrod, in his possessive mood of late, would undoubtedly have suspected his brother's motives. She wasn't too sure of them herself, not after her birthday party when he had expressed such an interest in her himself. And she had to admit that he was very attractive.

"Yes," was the only answer she gave to his statement.

Dave laughed. "Hey, don't you start getting suspicious on me, too. I've been meaning to come over and see you for days now. I would have been over earlier tonight but I had to work late at the last minute. Perhaps it was as well I was later than I expected to be."

"Because of Jarrod?"

"Mmm. He's been very clamlike and possessive about his relationship with you. I've tried to talk to him several times about you but he always changes the subject."

"Probably because there's nothing to tell," she evaded.

"Oh, come on, you're the interest of the year in his crowd—the girl to capture Jarrod Stone. That's no mean task, let me tell you."

"I wouldn't exactly say I've captured him," she denied quickly. "We are engaged, yes. But an engagement doesn't mean that much nowadays."

Dave's interest quickened. "Does that mean what I hope it means?"

Brooke's blue eyes never flickered once. "What do you hope it means?"

"That you and Jarrod are breaking up."

"I don't think that's the normal reaction of the brother of the engaged man. Or is it just that you don't approve of me for Jarrod?" She had sensed Dave's reluctance about them ever since she had first been introduced to him.

"For Jarrod, no—for me, yes."

She gave an amazed laugh. "Dave!" Humor wrestled with shock, and it was humor that finally won. "How can you say such things?" she chuckled.

"It's the way I feel. The more I think about it the more I wish I'd met you first."

"You're sure it's not just a case of wanting something that belongs to your brother?"

His candid blue eyes narrowed. "And do you—belong to my brother I mean?"

She blushed. "We're engaged, so in a way I suppose I do." According to Jarrod she belonged to him completely. Her mouth tightened at the thought of him.

Dave didn't miss that look. "You don't exactly

look ecstatic about that. And your engagement wasn't what I meant and you know it. I wondered if anything had changed since you were at the house together.''

The subject was embarrassing to Brooke and she wished he wouldn't pursue it. Things could have been very different for her and Jarrod by now if she had just verbally admitted how much she wanted and needed him instead of just physically capitulating. They could have been married by now and she wouldn't have these constant partings from him. The more she thought about it the more she wondered at herself for holding out against him. Pride, that's what it was, just pride. And pride was a poor bedfellow.

''Well, we still haven't decided on our wedding date if that's what you mean,'' she deliberately misunderstood him.

''You're being deliberately obtuse, you must have been taking lessons from Jarrod.''

She had been taking lessons from Jarrod, but not the sort he meant! ''I'm not being obtuse, Dave. There are just some things that are too private to talk about.''

''I see.'' He chewed his bottom lip thoughtfully. ''And has Jarrod seen any more of the beautiful Mrs. Howard?''

''How would I know?'' she asked sharply. She had wondered the same thing herself, but as they had seen each other every night for the last two weeks she didn't think he could have had much opportunity. But where there was a will there was a way....

''I really like you, Brooke,'' Dave said gently. ''And I wouldn't like my big brother to hurt you in any way. If he's being faithful to you it will be the first time he's been faithful to any woman in his life.''

She gave a bitter smile. ''That's what I like, brotherly loyalty.''

Dave had the grace to flush a little. ''All's fair in love and war.''

"I don't think this could be called either of those things, not between the two of us, anyway."

"But with Jarrod it's different," he said resignedly. "If he feels that way about you why don't the two of you get married and stop putting temptation in my way. Or could it be that Jarrod is still holding out on actually getting married?"

Brooke shook her head. "I'm sorry to disappoint you, Dave, but I'm the one holding out."

"You are?" He didn't attempt to hide his surprise.

She nodded. "Jarrod would get married tomorrow if I would agree to it. But marriage is the ultimate and I want to be very sure before I make any definite agreement."

"So you aren't sure?" he persisted eagerly.

She couldn't help laughing at his impetuosity, his complete lack of guile. She could imagine Jarrod had been very like Dave at this age, that once he had seen something he wanted he wouldn't rest until he got it. Maturity had given him a more subtle approach. And he used it shamelessly.

"I'm sure I love him, I'm just not sure a marriage between us would work," she stood up, a tiny figure in her denims and checked shirt, her reddish brown hair tumbling in disorder down her slender back. "I'll make us some coffee."

"Playing safe?" he quirked a mocking eyebrow.

"I am safe. Would you like some coffee? It's only instant I'm afraid."

"That will be fine. So you don't consider me a threat to Jarrod at all?" He looked disappointed, like a little boy denied a treat.

"I'm afraid not," she told him gently. "But I could do with a friend."

He looked sulky. "It wasn't what I had in mind."

She chuckled. "I'm sure it wasn't." She went out into the kitchen.

She moved around the room with a familiarity that

was habitual, preparing the tray with the coffee cups, humming to herself as she worked. She placed the tray on the coffee table in front of him. "Would you like something to eat? I don't suppose you've eaten if you came here straight from work."

"I had something at about four-thirty, but I could eat a sandwich if it's not too much trouble." He took the coffee cup she handed him.

"No trouble at all. Ham and tomato all right?"

"Fine. But drink your coffee first."

"It won't take me two minutes. Are you sure you wouldn't prefer something a little more substantial? I have some steaks in the refrigerator. I could do you chips and peas with it," she added temptingly.

He licked his lips at the sound of the appetizing meal, slowly shaking his head. "You live well. I can't even afford mince let alone steak."

"I bought the steaks because I thought Jarrod was staying to dinner," she told him honestly. "As a matter of fact I haven't had dinner myself, yet."

"In that case get cooking." He smiled with relish. "I shall enjoy eating the food intended for Jarrod."

She grinned. "I thought you might."

She wasn't a good cook but she could peel potatoes and get the chips cooking and open a packet of frozen peas with the best of them. The steaks were even simpler to cook and within twenty minutes she had the steaming hot meal on the table.

Dave's eyes lit up at the sight of the food and although he professed to be only moderately hungry he despatched the food with consummate ease. Brooke opened a tin of cream to go with the apple pie she had and he ate this with similar gusto.

He sat back with a sigh of satisfaction. "That was lovely. I could do with someone like you cooking for me full time."

"There wasn't much cooking involved. You could make yourself a meal like that if you wanted to. But

I'm the same when I'm on my own, it just doesn't seem worth cooking for one. And I don't think, at this stage in your career, that a wife would be a good idea." She began to clear away the debris from the meal.

He raised one dark eyebrow. "Who said anything about a wife?"

"But I thought— Oh, I see what you mean." Her nose wrinkled up with disgust.

Dave chuckled at her expression. "I thought you would. No wonder Jarrod finds you fascinating, your naiveté is charming. This is the age of the permissive society, or didn't you know that?"

"Does that mean we all have to forget our morals and jump into bed with anyone we care to?" she snapped, stung by his taunting tone. She marched out to the tiny kitchen and began to wash up noisily.

Dave had followed her out, shifting from one foot to the other as she continued to ignore him. "Hey, I didn't mean to annoy you. It's just that most of the kids I know indulge in casual affairs."

She determinedly didn't look at him, handing him the cloth to dry the draining dishes. He had helped make them dirty so he could help with the work, too. "Including you?" she asked through stiff lips.

He was very red faced. "Well, I...I...it's expected of a man!" he said defensively.

"Oh, yes!" Brooke agreed scathingly. "Don't say any more, I've heard it all before."

"Hey look where do you come off preaching to me?" he asked nastily. "You might look prim enough but I actually saw you in bed with my brother. The whole family knew about it."

She stopped what she was doing to glare at him. "Jarrod explained to your mother exactly what had happened," she said fiercely.

Dave looked equally as angry. "Oh, yes, the nightmare you were supposed to have had. I doubt if it was true, you probably sleep with Jarrod all the time. It would be so easy to invent something like a nightmare to fool my parents."

"Why you—"

He threw the cloth down. "You can't deny the evidence, Brooke. I saw you in my brother's arms, saw the possessive hold he had on you as if you had been together like that a lot."

Her hand moved up as if in slow motion to slap him hard across the face. She was surprised at her action but not repentant. "Don't judge everyone by your own rules," she told him tautly.

He removed his hand from his stinging cheek, revealing the bright red weals on his face. His expression couldn't be called pleasant. "There was no need for you to do that," he said grimly. "But I'll give you reason now." He took a threatening step toward her.

Brooke was becoming frightened, now. This wasn't the Dave who had entered her apartment, but a man with grim determination on his face. She backed away from him as far as she was able in the small confines of her kitchen. "Don't be silly, Dave," she trembled. "You'll regret this."

"I might do. But on the other hand it might be worth it. You have to possess something more than beauty to hold on to Jarrod."

"I don't think your opinion of Jarrod is any more complimentary than the one you have of me."

By this time he had her firmly pinned against the wall. "I respect and love Jarrod more than anyone else I've ever known," he contradicted. "He's everything I ever want to be." One of his hands moved to caress her suddenly pale cheeks.

"I see. I suppose it's all this love and respect you have for him that's making you make a pass at his fiancée," she scorned, more frightened than she cared to admit. Dave was almost as well built and muscular as Jarrod, and he had an equal amount of determination.

"No," he disagreed mildly. "It's you that's making me do that, you with your coolness that makes me want to melt you until you're on fire for me." His mouth tightened. "As Jarrod has no doubt seen you any amount of times."

She blushed. It was true, Jarrod had seen her like that, aroused and aflame with wanting him. "You... you're mad! Jarrod will kill you for this."

He shook his head, a slight smile on his lips. "Jarrod will never know."

"Oh, yes he will! I—"

"Won't tell him," he finished for her. "Because if you did I would have to tell him that you invited me over here this evening, encouraging me until it became impossible for me to refuse you."

"He wouldn't believe you." But there was a ring of uncertainty in her voice, a fact Dave was quick to notice.

"Would you like to risk it?" he murmured, lowering his head to caress her throat with his mouth.

She squirmed away from him. "Please, don't do this, Dave. Please," she pleaded.

He didn't answer her, pulling her fully into his arms and claiming possession of her lips. Brooke could have found the locality of this attack amusing if she wasn't quite so annoyed. Dave certainly hadn't chosen the most romantic of places to try and seduce her, surrounded by dirty dishes as they were.

As if sensing this, with a dexterity that surprised her, he had led her into the lounge, lying beside her on the sofa. Their closeness reminded her poignantly of Jarrod and other evenings when he had strained her to him with equal passion.

Dave was very like Jarrod to look at and it was easy to imagine that the lips demanding a response from her own were his, that he was right here with her and not out with a business colleague, if indeed that's where he was.

She was no longer fighting Dave, but she wasn't responding, either, lying quietly in his arms as he further explored her creamy throat. That he was fully roused she knew by the hardness of his thighs and yet the knowledge didn't repulse her. It would be so easy to imagine him as Jarrod and give in to the longing that always enveloped her whenever she was in his arms.

"I want you, Brooke," Dave murmured throatily.

"Unfortunately, so do I," remarked a quietly controlled voice from above them. "And I believe I have first claim to her."

Dave had shot up off the sofa at the first sound of his brother's voice. "Jarrod! What are you doing here?"

Brooke could have asked him the same question but on seeing the dangerous glitter in his eyes she was glad she hadn't. He hadn't looked at her, yet, his anger was all centered on Dave at the moment. She sat up dazedly on the sofa, watching the two of them as if they were strangers to her.

Jarrod came farther into the room, removing the black bow tie he had been wearing, unbuttoning the top two buttons of his shirt before removing his jacket, a cold hard look on his face.

He looked at his younger brother. "The same thing as you I should imagine," he answered curtly. "But Brooke should remember when she has invited one lover to spend the night with her before inviting another. It could prove embarrassing—for her," he added harshly.

She gasped at his words. "But, Jarrod, I—"

"Weren't expecting me back just yet?" he finished for her, sitting down in one of the armchairs to look at the two of them interestedly, only the slate gray of his eyes showing just how furious he really was. "I know that. I would say it was pretty obvious," he said grimly.

Dave looked at Brooke, disgust written all over his face. "Did you know Jarrod was coming back here tonight?" he demanded of her.

"Well, I—"

"Of course she did," interrupted Jarrod. "I stay here most nights now." He smiled but it couldn't be called a pleasant smile. "I'm trying to pursuade Brooke that she would be a fool not to marry me."

"If you ask me you would be the fool." Dave turned on his heel and walked toward the door. "She didn't put up much of a fight when I kissed her."

"That isn't—"

Suddenly Jarrod was standing up, a menacing figure glowering down at them. "*You* kissed *her*, did you?" he asked, dangerously soft.

Dave realized his mistake too late, paling at the unhidden danger in his brother's eyes. "Well, I...I..." he blustered, reaching hurriedly for the doorknob. "I may have done," he continued defiantly. "But she didn't fight me," he repeated.

Brooke had heard enough. They were like two animals fighting over a mate. But she had to admit that the cool intensity of Jarrod's anger was quite frightening. And she would have to bear the brunt of it when Dave had left.

"Don't lie on top of everything else, Dave," she said sharply. "You threatened me."

"With what?" Jarrod queried softly of his brother.

Dave looked even more unsure of himself and Brooke began to feel sorry for him. If they hadn't been interrupted the incident between them might have passed off quite easily, but Jarrod turning up in this way had made a big issue out of it.

"With what, Dave?" he repeated harshly.

Dave gave a nervous laugh. "I didn't threaten her

with anything," he lied. "Look, Brooke gave me dinner, does that sound as if I threatened her?"

Jarrod shrugged. "You tell me."

"Well, I didn't," Dave maintained firmly. "Now if you'll excuse me I have to be back on duty at seven o'clock in the morning. Thanks for the meal, Brooke."

Brooke looked at Jarrod with pleading eyes once Dave had left. "It wasn't the way he made it sound," she said desperately. "I did give him a meal, yes, but I didn't encourage him to kiss me."

He looked at her coldly. "When you invite a man around for a meal you must expect to invite him around for something else, too."

"I didn't *invite* him here at all," she declared vehemently. "He just turned up."

"Oh, really?"

"Yes, really." His sarcasm hadn't gone unnoticed. "Don't you believe me?"

"Why shouldn't I?" He flexed his shoulder muscles. "The one night I have to leave you in two weeks and Dave just turned up here unexpectedly. I quite understand that it was on the off chance that he turned up here."

"But it was! Please believe me, Jarrod. We even laughed at the fact that Dave had just missed you. He said how lucky..." she broke off as she realized her frantic pleadings were just making things worse.

"How lucky that I had already left," he murmured softly. "But I came back and ruined it all for you."

"*Why* did you come back?"

He threw back his head and gave a harsh laugh. "I'm not sure now."

Brooke's eyes were violet in her distress. She was going to lose Jarrod on the evening she had decided to marry him! She had decided that if he wanted her enough to marry her she wanted him enough to agree.

"But there must have been a reason for it. You said when you left earlier that you would see me tomorrow."

He gave a deep sigh, impatiently watching the nervous movements of her hands. "Oh, there was a reason for my coming back," he agreed coldly. "I came back for you."

She looked at him sharply. "For...for *me*?"

"Yes," he said, again with that harsh laugh. "How did you expect me to concentrate on talking business after the stormy scene we had just shared? I made my excuses as soon as it was polite to do so and came straight back here," his mouth hardened. "Only to find you in my brother's arms."

"It wasn't like it seemed. He—"

"If I had realized my constantly arousing you but not giving you the satisfaction you craved, would lead you to seeking that satisfaction with another man I would have taken you long ago. As it is—" he took a threatening step toward her "—I don't think it's too late for that—yet."

Brooke shrank away from the desire now flaming in his eyes. "You don't realize what you're doing, Jarrod. You're annoyed, I can understand that, but you're wrong about Dave and myself."

"Forget about Dave!" he ordered fiercely. "As long as you haven't gone any further with him than what I just witnessed I couldn't give a damn about him. Although it had better never be repeated." He swung her effortlessly into his arms, throwing her roughly down onto the bed once he reached her bedroom. "I told you I would have you begging for marriage, now I realize just how lenient I've been with you during the last few weeks, waiting for you to come to me willingly. Well, I'm not going to wait anymore. I want you, you want me, and by God I'm going to take you."

His hands on her body were not gentle and the

wildness in his eyes told her that the tight control he always had over his desire for her had finally snapped. She had pushed him too far and would now have to pay the penalty.

He wasted no time in unbuttoning her shirt, ripping the material as he ruthlessly pulled it apart. Several of the buttons came off altogether, but Jarrod ignored them, once again devouring her flesh devoid of underwear.

She struggled against him. "Please, Jarrod!" she cried. "I know you're angry with me, but not like this. *Please.*"

"I'm not angry with you, Brooke. I'm bloody furious!" He continued to kiss and caress her.

She pushed at his body on her own, knowing only pain and humiliation in his arms this time. "You have a right to be, I admit that. But I can't let you make love to me. When you wanted to marry me it was different, but now that's over I—"

That made him lift his head. "Who said it was over? Oh, no, Brooke, you aren't getting away that easily. For weeks now people have been asking me when our wedding is to be, mainly due to your bitchiness in broadcasting it at that party simply because you felt I was making a fool of you. Well, now I can tell them exactly when we're getting married. Three weeks tomorrow you're going to become my wife."

CHAPTER EIGHT

"I...I AM?"

"Yes, you damn well are!"

"But you...you can't still want me to marry you, not after...."

He gave a tight smile, some of the tense anger seeming to leave his body. "I still want you, and I still have to convince Charles Howard that I'm much too interested in my own woman to want his. They were the reasons for the marriage in the first place and they haven't changed." His grip tightened painfully on her arms. "But if I ever find you in another man's arms once we're married I'll kill you—after I've dealt with him, of course."

There was a dangerous edge to his voice that told her he meant exactly what he said. "Of course," she said dryly.

Jarrod got up off the bed, turning to look at her with narrowed eyes. "As long as you realize that." He ran a hand through his already tousled black hair. "Get something on for God's sake!" he snapped abruptly, marching back out into the lounge.

She did so with jerky movements, removing the ruined shirt altogether and putting on a yellow T-shirt. She came out of the bedroom smoothing the top down over her narrow hips. "Might I remind you that it was you who ripped at my clothing like a...like a—"

"An animal?" he queried softly, a stiff measure of whiskey in his hand. Not normally a drinker herself she had bought the bottle especially for Jarrod when she realized how much he appreciated it when he came here in the evenings.

"Yes!" Her eyes flashed. "And then you have the nerve to talk to me as if I'm—"

"A wanton?" he finished for her again.

"Yes!" she said vehemently.

"Then that makes us well matched. I see you've kept Angie's present to you," he remarked suddenly.

"I'm sorry?" she evaded.

"The portrait in your bedroom."

"Oh, that," she dismissed casually. "I had to keep it really, it would have been rude not to."

"But did you have to put it in your bedroom?"

She gave a short laugh. "The lounge didn't seem the ideal place. I didn't particularly want you looming down at all my guests."

He threw the remainder of the whiskey in his glass to the back of his throat, swallowing it without a wince. "Then I'm surprised you chose your bedroom," he said nastily.

"Why you...!"

"Yes?" he asked softly. "Can't you stand to hear the truth?"

"The truth as you see it?" She shook her head. "No, I can't stand to listen to your biased opinion of me. Just because you've forced yourself into my bedroom a couple of times doesn't mean other men have been in there." She ripped off the ring that seemed to be more like a chain with every passing second. "Take your ring and get out of here!"

"We're getting married," he stated adamantly.

"I wouldn't marry you under any circumstances!" she lied. If he loved her she would marry him tomorrow, but his contempt she wouldn't put up with.

He moved toward her. "Are you sure about that?" he asked seductively soft.

"Very sure," she answered firmly. "And making

love to me won't work this time," she denied, forcing herself not to move as he stood a few inches away from her. "You aren't that good a lover, Jarrod. Dave's just as good as you are, with much less practice I would say."

"You think so?" He jerked her chin up roughly. "So things had gone further between you than I thought they had. How often does Dave come here?"

"Whenever he can." Which was true, according to Dave this had been the first opportunity he had had to call on her.

He picked up his discarded jacket. "You little bitch!" he stated calmly. "Keep the ring, Dave will never be able to afford one like it."

"Oh, we don't intend to get married."

"You have discussed it then?"

"We have talked of marriage, yes. But it isn't for us, not to each other, anyway." How could she talk so calmly when what she really wanted to do was launch herself into his arms?

"So you would have married me while having an affair with my own brother?"

"Must I remind you that I have never at any time said I would marry you. But even if I had you have every intention of carrying on your affair with Mrs. Howard."

"That's—"

"Different?" she cut in. "It may seem that way to you but I wouldn't have liked it."

"So you had an affair with my brother," he repeated.

"Yes," she answered because it seemed to be what he expected of her.

"I once said you were full of surprises," he said bitterly. "I just didn't realize how much."

"Goodbye, Jarrod," she said dully.

"Goodbye." The door closed with a slam.

Well, she had done it now, alienated Jarrod beyond

repair. But it had been the only course open to her when he could think such things of her. She couldn't marry a man who had such a contemptuous opinion of her. It would have been hell on earth, with her having to pay for every past indiscretion he believed her guilty of. No matter what Jarrod did himself he wouldn't want a wife who had had affairs with other men, his wife would have to be beyond reproach. And in his eyes she certainly wasn't that now!

THE WEEKEND now loomed before her like a black empty void. Jarrod may only have been in her life a matter of weeks but during that time he had effectively cut off any of her other social life, making it impossible for her to meet any of her other friends.

She woke up Saturday morning with a feeling of dread for the weekend, especially tonight. No one stayed in on a Saturday night, and most of her friends would already have made plans for the evening.

But by midafternoon she had had enough of her tiny apartment, feeling as if the walls were closing in around her. She had to get out, go *somewhere* this evening. She just had to!

A call to a couple of her friends confirmed that a crowd of them were going to a nightclub that evening and they were only too happy to invite her along. She had missed going out with the crowd, missed their comradery and good humor. She and four other girls had become good friends during the time she had stayed at a hostel and although they had all left to make their own homes they still kept in touch with each other.

Debbie and Lynnette called for her in their taxi, none of them wanting to risk driving after an evening spent drinking. Both of her friends were agog with curiosity about what had happened to that "tall hunk of a fiancé of hers." Neither girl had ever met Jarrod Stone but like most people they had seen photographs of him in the society columns.

The three girls left their wraps in the cloakroom, making their way over to the booked table next to the dance floor, the band already providing music for half a dozen couples smooching around the floor.

Not having explained her suddenly free evening Brooke knew she would come in for a certain amount of questioning—and it wasn't long in coming. As they were the first of their party to arrive it gave the other two girls time to question her in private.

"So what happened to your engagement?" Debbie looked pointedly at her bare left hand, the ring that had adorned the third finger now locked away out of sight. "Surely you didn't change your mind?"

Brooke sipped her dry Martini and lemonade. "It was a mutual thing. We just decided we weren't suited."

Lynnette looked at her wide-eyed. "Goodness, I would have made sure I suited a dreamboat like him. He's gorgeous."

Brooke gave a distant smile. She had known there would be questions like this, even more so when she went into work on Monday, but it didn't make them hurt any less. No matter what she may have to tell other people about the end of her engagement—she loved Jarrod.

"He is very handsome, yes," she agreed, pretending an interest in the band she didn't have, even though they were exceptionally good.

The place was beginning to fill up and in an hour or so's time what was now an almost empty dance floor would be overflowing with people. Perhaps then she wouldn't be the focus of her friends' interest, although she couldn't really blame them for their curiosity, one minute she was engaged to Jarrod and the next he wasn't even speaking to her.

"Handsome!" scoffed Debbie. "He's fantastic," she corrected her. "He has beautiful, sexy, smoldering gray eyes. I saw a picture of him in a magazine a few weeks ago. I couldn't believe how lucky you were when I saw you were engaged to him."

"Thank you for your card by the way." Brooke sighed. "But those smoldering sexy eyes can also be contemptuous and glacial as snow. Believe me," she shuddered. "I know."

"Oh, but surely he wasn't like that with you," Lynnette gasped.

"Don't you believe it. No, Jarrod is a very handsome exciting man, but he's also a ruthless one. I'm afraid I'm not up to being the perfect wife." Far from it in Jarrod's eyes!

"I think it's a shame. Still, as long as you aren't too brokenhearted about it." Debbie looked at her sympathetically, obviously doubting the truth of that.

Brooke shrugged. "I'm upset, naturally. No one likes to admit they made a mistake, but it was better to find out now than after we were married. I just realized I didn't fit in with his idea of a wife." She had definitely never been the complacent sort and she wasn't about to become so in marriage, and Jarrod needed a wife who would accept his affairs with other women.

When the rest of their crowd arrived ten minutes later, they were just as curious, but they were given the same vague excuses as Debbie and Lynnette and had to be satisfied with that. There were two more girls as Sheila had brought along a friend of hers from work, and there were six boys. They were all known to Brooke and she soon found herself laughing and joking with them in the old way, thoughts of Jarrod pushed firmly to the back of her mind.

"You're really finished with this guy Stone?" asked Jerry, an American student over here studying English history.

Brooke turned to look at him, sobering slightly at the mention of Jarrod's name. "I'm no longer engaged to him," she confirmed.

"Temporarily or permanently?"

She frowned. "I don't understand."

Jerry grinned, a tall loose-limbed man with over-long blond hair and a winning smile. He and Brooke had dated a couple of times in the past but nothing had ever come of it. "What I mean is, are you finished for good or is this just a momentary disagreement, you know a lovers' tiff?"

"Definitely the former."

"Good," he said with some satisfaction, giving a bashful grin at her shocked look. "Sorry, honey, that was a purely selfish viewpoint."

"Selfish?"

"Mmm." He took a large gulp of his whiskey. "We had dated a couple of times just before you got engaged to this guy and I was pretty surprised when you suddenly decided to marry him. I was quite interested in you myself, you know."

"You were?"

"Yes, I was—I still am. I realize you're probably upset at the moment, but I could help you get over that a whole lot quicker."

"You could?" she asked with a smile, starting to relax a bit now. This was the sort of man she could handle, the sort of man she felt at ease with. It seemed that only with the Stone men did she feel that muscle-tightening feeling of fear and anticipation. She had been right to feel both emotions.

"Oh, yes," he stood up, pulling her to her feet. "We'll start by dancing together."

Before she could protest he had pulled her onto the dance floor, holding her closely against his body as they moved to the slow music. They laughed and talked as they danced and only returned to the table to drink thirstily. It was warm work trying to survive among that crowd although it wasn't long before they went back again.

As it happened to be a fast moving number they

danced away from each other, Brooke becoming lost
in the music. She felt quite exhausted at the end of it
and collapsed thankfully into Jerry's arms, laughing
happily up at him.

It was at just this moment, her head thrown back,
her eyes violet with pleasure, her smile for Jerry
alone, that she saw the couple just stepping onto the
dance floor for the next dance—Jarrod and Selina
Howard! And Jarrod was looking at *her* with undis-
guised contempt.

She looked quickly away, all color leaving her face.
"Would you mind if we sat down, Jerry?" she asked
breathlessly.

He put an arm around her shoulders. "That last one
wore you out, did it?" he teased.

She gave a shaky smile. "Yes."

She deliberately swapped seats with Jerry, her back
now firmly turned to the couple she most wanted to
avoid. How dare Jarrod come here so blatantly with
that woman! She boiled inside, not hearing a word
Jerry said.

"Brooke?" he touched her hand.

"Yes?" she asked sharply. She smiled at him
wanly. "Sorry, Jerry, I think I have a headache coming on."

"Would you like me to take you home?"

There was nothing she would like better but it
would be too much like running away. No, she would
stay here and act as if nothing had happened. She gave
Jerry a dazzling smile. "Another drink will soon clear
my head."

"Sure it will." He stopped a waiter and ordered the
required drinks. "You haven't had enough to make
you feel relaxed, yet."

Until a few moments ago she had been completely
relaxed and enjoying herself immensely. Until she
had seen Jarrod that is. Oh, damn Jarrod and the attraction she still felt toward him.

"Here you are." Jerry handed her a cool drink. "Get that down you and you'll soon forget you ever had a headache."

As she hadn't had one to start with that was highly likely. Nevertheless, after this she threw herself more enthusiastically into the enjoyment of the evening, electing to stay on with Jerry after the others decided they had had enough. Debbie and Lynnette were a trifle reluctant about leaving her but Jerry assured them he would see her home safely.

"I thought they would never leave," Jerry pulled her to her feet. "Let's dance."

And dance they did, for what seemed like hours—and probably was. Occasionally she looked around the room for a sight of Jarrod, but she could see him nowhere. Perhaps he had already left; it was possible.

At twelve-thirty she excused herself. She was feeling hot and sticky and wanted to brush her hair and freshen up her makeup. Luckily she had chosen to wear a cool, flowing flower-printed dress, sleeveless, with a low neckline that revealed the dark shadow between her breasts.

Her hair brushed back into some semblance of glowing order and her lipstick reapplied she left the powder room to return to their table. She didn't get very far, a firm grip on her arm stopping her progress. She looked up from that familiar looking hand into the grim face of Jarrod Stone. So he hadn't left after all!

"What do you think you're playing at?" he snapped harshly with no preliminaries.

Brooke blinked rapidly at this verbal attack on her. "What do you mean?"

"Don't play games with me," he said in a controlled voice. "Just what do you mean by coming here with your boyfriend tonight?"

"Why shouldn't I?" She snatched her wrist out of his grasp, causing extra pain to herself as he didn't want to let go. "You don't have a monopoly on this place."

"I don't have the monopoly on it but I do partly own it."

"I should have guessed," she said dryly. "Does this mean you're asking me to leave?"

"Not at all, it means I want to know who your friend is."

Her eyes sparkled with anger. "It's none of your business, nothing I do is now."

A cruel smile curved that firm mouth. "I think it is," he insisted determinedly. "I haven't refuted our engagement, yet, and it could prove rather embarrassing for us both if you're spotted here with another man."

She stood proud, her head thrown back. "And who would I be spotted by? I'm not exactly a well-known face. Unless of course your companion sees me. But I can't really see that that would make any difference, she already knows our engagement was a sham."

He frowned. "My companion? And who might that be?"

"Now who's playing games," she scorned. "Let me go, Jarrod. Jerry will be wondering where I am."

"So his name's Jerry," he said softly. "Have you known him long?"

"Long enough."

"For what?"

"For whatever," she answered carelessly.

"I see,", his mouth tightened. "Now perhaps you'll tell me what game *I'm* supposed to be playing?"

"I saw you with that woman so don't try to deny it. I think you should be the one to worry if you're seen with *her*, not me."

"By 'that woman' I presume you mean Selina. Does it bother you that I'm here with her?"

At last he let go of her wrist and she glowered at him as she massaged the reddened skin. "Why should

I care? I've always known she came first in your life so why should it bother me if you see her?''

"You tell me.''

"It *doesn't* bother me,'' she said crossly. "Excuse me, but I would like to rejoin my friend.'' She turned on her heel and walked away, expecting at any moment to feel his hand on her arm. When it didn't happen she didn't know if she was relieved or disappointed.

Whatever her emotions were she became quite recklessly enthusiastic about the evening, drinking heavily between dances. Jerry was becoming quite friendly, but in her state of rejection she didn't seem to mind his attentions, Jarrod may no longer want her but she was still attractive to other men; Jerry made it clear that he found her very attractive.

She swallowed the remainder of her drink, about her seventh of the evening. "Shall we dance again?'' she asked him gaily.

"Sure,'' he agreed readily.

The music had slowed down a little with the progression of the evening and she snuggled against him as they danced. It may not be the best reason for her to be in his arms but for now it was the only one she had. He was quite good-looking and she badly needed a salve to her dented ego at the moment. Besides, he was fun to be with.

They danced close together, their bodies curved together as they moved to the music. Jerry bent his head to caress her throat with demanding lips. "Can we leave soon, honey?'' he asked huskily.

"Soon,'' she promised. "But it's early, yet.''

"It's after two in the morning,'' he corrected. "I don't call that early.''

Brooke pouted up at him. "Don't be a meany. You don't have to get up for college in the morning.''

"I wasn't thinking about the morning,'' he murmured, his eyes admiring. "When can I take you home?''

She looked at him reproachfully. "We have plenty of time to go home. I'm enjoying myself."

"So am I," he brushed his lips across her mouth. "But I can think of a way I would enjoy myself more."

She giggled. "That's naughty."

"I know, but I—"

"Excuse me!" A harshly angry voice interrupted their conversation.

Brooke turned with dazed eyes to see Jarrod standing at her side. She and Jerry had stopped dancing at the first sound of his voice, jerked out of their flirtatious mood by the coldness of his tone. Brooke felt sure he must have heard part of their bantering conversation and she knew what construction he would have put on it.

Jerry looked at the other man challengingly. "Yeah? Can I do something for you?"

Jarrod gave him a glacial look. "Not you, no. I would like to talk to Brooke."

"She's with me." Jerry had had as much to drink as she had and it had given him more courage than he might otherwise have had. "So anything you have to say can be said in front of me."

He received a look of arrogant disdain for his rude outburst. "I don't think so," Jarrod disagreed. "What I have to say to Brooke is totally private."

"We don't have any secrets from each other."

Even Brooke looked sharply at Jerry for this statement. They may have dated a couple of times but they had never been *that* close. Still, she couldn't altogether blame Jerry for his defiant attitude, Jarrod brought out those feelings in her, too. It was all that arrogance that did it.

Jarrod gave a nasty smile. "What I have to say to Brooke isn't exactly a secret, I should think everyone in the club has been thinking what I'm about to say."

Brooke bristled angrily. "What do you mean?"

"Could we go to your table and sit down?" Jarrod suggested. "We're rather conspicuous standing here."

For the first time she became aware of how they must look to other people, standing here in the middle of a crowded dance floor having an obviously hostile conversation. She nodded distantly, her gaiety of a few minutes earlier gone completely.

"Now," Jarrod leaned forward in his chair. "You're making an exhibition of yourself," he told her coldly. "I could almost say you're drunk."

"Why you—"

"And as for you," he cut into Jerry's indignant outburst. "If you don't stop pawing her I'm going to kill you!"

The words were spoken so softly and with such force that Brooke knew he meant it. Surely Jarrod couldn't be jealous? If only he were!

Jerry seemed to have got over his surprise at such a statement and now gave an assured smile. "Perhaps the lady likes to be pawed," he drawled.

"Maybe she does," Jarrod acknowledged. "But if anyone is going to paw her it's going to be me. Brooke is my fiancée."

Jerry looked impressed. "So you're Jarrod Stone."

"That's right. So you can understand why I'm not too pleased at seeing her here with you."

"Oh, I can understand it, but as Brooke claims to be no longer engaged to you I don't think it's any of your concern now."

Brooke gasped. "I don't *claim* anything. I'm not—"

"We have had a temporary setback, that's all," Jarrod declared firmly. "She's only here with you to hit back at me."

Jerry grinned. "She seems to have succeeded."

Jarrod gave a wry smile. "Doesn't she just. So in the circumstances I hope you will understand my wanting to take her home now," he said smoothly.

"I don't want—"

"Neither do I, honey." Jerry hadn't been fooled by the now charming manner of this man, remembering the threat he had made and the conviction behind the words. "Brooke came with me," he lied. "And she's leaving with me."

Gray eyes raked over him mercilessly. "Are you sure about that?"

Jerry stood up, taking Brooke with him. "Very sure. It's been...interesting meeting you, Mr. Stone. No, don't bother to see us to the door, we know the way out."

Brooke collected up her handbag, halted once again by Jarrod's grip on her arm. "Let go of me," she ordered.

"I want to talk to you, Brooke."

"We've said all we had to say." She held up her left hand. "You see, I no longer wear your brand of possession."

"Does Dave know about your new boyfriend?"

She shrugged, forgetting her earlier declaration that she was having an affair with his brother. "Why should he? No one *owns* me."

"Then perhaps it's time someone did," he said softly. "Good night."

"Good night," she answered, startled by his sudden turnabout of mood.

He looked at Jerry again. "I take it you're not going to attempt to drive?"

"And if I were?" Jerry asked insolently.

Jarrod shrugged. "I would simply make a telephone call to the police informing them of your inebriated state."

"Thanks!" Jerry returned dryly. "But as I don't possess a car that won't be necessary." He put his arm around Brooke's shoulders. "Good night, Mr. Stone."

Jarrod didn't answer but turned on his heel and walked away. Brooke was still shaking from the encounter when she returned to Jerry's side after collecting her wrap. They got into a waiting taxi, Jerry giving the driver Brooke's address.

He turned to her in the darkness of the car. "A very determined man, your Mr. Stone," he remarked.

"He isn't my Mr. Stone," she answered crossly.

"He doesn't seem to be of the same opinion."

"He just wanted to be nasty."

Jerry shook his head. "I don't think so. He was mad as hell to see you in my arms."

"Not through jealousy, I can assure you."

"Hey, come on, Brooke, there's no need to get aggressive with me. I'm only telling you that the guy didn't like you being with me. If we hadn't been in such a public place he would probably have hit me. And that was no idle threat he made about my touching you."

She knew that, and instead of the elated feeling she had felt all evening she now felt thoroughly depressed, craving only her own company.

"I guess you would prefer me not to come in for coffee," Jerry said as the taxi came to a halt outside her apartment.

She was grateful for his understanding. "Thanks, Jerry. Some other time, hmm? Call me."

"Sure." He leaned forward and kissed her softly on the lips. "Good night, honey."

She went straight into the bathroom when she got in, running the water for a shower before going into the bedroom to remove her clothes. The effects of the alcohol were beginning to wear off and her temples throbbed.

The warm water helped to ease her pain somewhat but it couldn't alleviate her humiliation. Jarrod had made her evening with Jerry seem cheap, and reluctant as she was to admit it, he was right. She had made a fool of herself tonight, an absolute fool.

Her hair tied on top of her head with a black velvet

ribbon and a towel secured around her body at her breasts she came back into the bedroom totally refreshed. The sight that met her eyes made her cheeks pale even more.

"Jarrod!" she gasped as she saw him sprawled full length on her bed. "What are you doing here?"

He slowly sat up, his eyes appraising as he gazed boldly at her body. "Waiting for you. What else would I be doing?"

CHAPTER NINE

"W-WAITING FOR ME?" she repeated breathlessly.

He stood up now, coming toward her. "Mmm," he murmured. "Your eyes were promising things tonight I have no intention of letting any other man collect."

"Promising things?" She clung to the towel that was in danger of falling off. "You...you're mistaken."

"I don't think so." He touched her pale cheeks. "You don't look well. Have you been ill?"

"No," she answered huskily, unnerved by his closeness.

"Not sick or anything? You've been drinking steadily all evening."

"I'm not drunk and I haven't been sick!" she snapped angrily, mainly as a defense against his blatant maleness than out of real anger. She hadn't expected to see him again tonight and she felt weakened by his presence in her bedroom.

"Then what's the matter with you? You look like death."

"Thanks." She moved jerkily away from his caressing hands. "I happen to have a headache." She heard him chuckle and turned to look at him. "What's so funny about that?"

"It's the classic excuse." His eyes were dark gray with amusement.

A strange fluttering sensation started in her stomach. "For what?"

"For not making love," he stated bluntly. "Is that why your boyfriend isn't here now?"

"Jerry isn't my boyfriend. And I have a much simpler way of avoiding making love. I just say no." Oh, God, she wished she had her bathrobe on, but it was still hanging on the back of the bathroom door. She felt so...so *naked* dressed only in this towel that barely reached her thighs.

He was right behind her now, his warm breath caressing her bare nape. "I have no intention of taking no from you tonight." His arms moved around her waist and he pulled her back against him, his hands possessively cupping her breasts. "I've come to collect, Brooke."

"Not from me, you haven't." She squirmed as his lips caressed her nape. "What's happened to your mistress tonight?" she sneered.

"Selina?" he murmured against her throat. "She's at home with her husband, I would imagine."

"Does he realize you were out with his wife this evening?" She gave up all effort of trying to escape him as he refused to let her go.

"Oh, yes, he knows." He continued a downward exploration of her creamy throat with his lips.

"Does he love his wife so much that he allows her to...to have men friends?" she asked in disgust, hoping to alienate him again by insulting him. She had to stop these caresses somehow.

"I have no idea of his feelings in the matter," he appeared unmoved by her sarcasm. "He was with us tonight, we were a party of eight. But I don't suppose you noticed that, you were too wrapped up in this Jerry."

Every time his lips touched her skin her heart gave a strange leap, and yet still she fought for sanity. "A party of eight," she said thoughtfully. "Who was your partner?"

He turned her in his arms to face him, holding her

against the lean length of him and making her wholly aware of his throbbing thighs. "A tall raven-haired beauty called Suzy."

"So if you aren't with your mistress why aren't you with this Suzy?" Her gaze was fixed on the third button down on his white shirt front.

He pretended shock. "Really, Brooke! I only met her for the first time this evening. Even I wouldn't presume so much on such short acquaintance."

"You surprise me."

He laughed. "I thought I might." He looked at her closely. "You look cute with your hair like that," he said softly. "But it's a cuteness that's totally deceptive." He pulled the ribbon free of her hair, allowing it to fall in glowing red waves around her shoulders. "You looked like a little girl with your hair like that and this isn't the time for me to be reminded of your youth."

His body pressed against her own was working its usual magic and her legs felt weak. And the lighting in this room didn't help the situation—one bedside lamp that added to the mood of seduction. "But I am young, Jarrod." She latched onto this point with desperation. "You can never change that."

"At this moment I don't want to change a single damn thing about you." He bent his head to claim her lips with his own.

She couldn't fight her own emotions anymore, couldn't fight the desire she felt for him. It had all been leading to this, all the arguments, all the friction. Her arms moved up around his neck and she gave up fighting him, revelling in his mastery of her.

"That was good," he groaned against her mouth. "I needed that. You did, too. Admit it."

"I—"

"Admit it, Brooke!"

"I needed it, too," she said softly.

He gave a triumphant laugh. As soon as he took his

arms from around her body the towel fell to the floor. It seemed to Brooke that her whole body suffused with color. She hurried to retrieve her only covering, but Jarrod stopped her.

"Leave it," he ordered, his eyes never leaving the perfection of her body. "God, you're more beautiful than even my imagination allowed for! Touching you isn't quite the same thing as seeing you like this." He took her hand, leading her over to the bed. "Undress me."

"No!" She felt awful standing here naked, even more so because Jarrod was totally dressed. "Let me get some clothes on, Jarrod," she pleaded.

"Oh, no," he sat her firmly down on the bed. "You can get under the covers if you like, but you are certainly not getting dressed, not now that I've got you this far."

She quickly did as he said, peering at him from below the safety of the sheet. He was calmly taking off his clothes as if they did this every night! Brooke looked hurriedly away as he stripped off his trousers, throwing them carelessly on the floor with his other clothes.

The next thing she knew the bed gave beside her and a pair of strong muscular arms pulled her against her first encounter with a naked male body. It felt good, really good, and she wondered if all men were as beautiful as Jarrod. She doubted it—he was just too perfect to be copied.

He was unique and her hands caressed him of their own volition. "This is wrong, Jarrod," she said breathlessly once he had released her lips, gasping as he touched her breasts.

"How can anything that feels so right possibly be wrong? It can't, Brooke," he answered his own question. "Can you deny that you want me?"

"No, but I—"

"Then it can't be wrong." He parted her lips with a

savagery that took her breath away, his hands moving intimately across her body.

Just when she thought that full possession was the only thing that would satisfy either of them the doorbell began to ring. It rang and rang until it finally penetrated even Jarrod's passion-filled brain.

He looked down at her with tortured eyes. "Are you expecting anyone?"

"No," she answered dazedly.

"Then who the hell is it!" He swore angrily as the doorbell continued to ring. He swung his legs out of the bed, pulling his trousers on before marching out furiously to open the door. Brooke pitied whoever it was.

She lay shivering in the bed in reaction, wondering at her own response and yet knowing she would respond just as passionately when he returned.

She could hear the murmur of voices in the lounge and wondered who Jarrod could possibly be talking to. She slipped out of the bed, grabbing her robe from the bathroom before quietly entering the lounge. Dave stood up at her entrance and Jarrod came over to put his arm around her shoulders, holding her protectively against his side.

She couldn't help noticing how pale they both were. "What's wrong?" she asked Jarrod. "Has something happened?"

His face was bleak. "My father has had a heart attack. I have to go to the hospital. Wait for me here while I dress," he told his brother before leaving the room.

Dave looked embarrassed. "Sorry to have burst in on you like this," he muttered.

"Is your father going to be all right?" she asked anxiously.

"They think so. Of course they can't be sure, yet. But I thought Jarrod ought to know."

"Oh, yes," she agreed. "I'm only relieved you thought to come here."

"I tried his apartment first, and then I tried a club

he occasionally goes to. It seems I just missed him at the club, so I tried his apartment again. He still wasn't there." He shrugged. "I couldn't think of anywhere else he could be. After all, he did say he spends a lot of his nights here."

"So he did," she agreed dully. "Excuse me, Dave. I have to speak to Jarrod."

"Hey," he stopped her exit. "I didn't mean to be insulting, you know. I was just trying to explain my reasoning."

She gave a wan smile. "I realize that. Now I must see Jarrod."

"Of course," he acknowledged.

Brooke gently touched his arm. "I told you how I felt about him from the beginning."

"Yes, you did. I'm sorry I tried to cause trouble between you yesterday."

If only he knew how much damage he had done! But he and Jarrod had enough to worry about with their father's illness without her raking up old arguments. She gave him a vague smile before rushing into her bedroom.

Jarrod was partly dressed by this time, his black leather shoes back on his feet and his shirt pulled back on over his powerful shoulders. His look darkened as she came into the room and she ran into his arms, her own arms passing around his waist below the unbuttoned shirt. She rested her head on his hair-roughened chest, aware of the strong steady beat of his heart.

He shuddered as her arms went around him, holding her close, his face buried in her luxurious hair. "God, this is a mess!" he moaned agonizingly.

She tilted her head back to look at him. "Your father will be all right. I'm sure he will." Her look was earnest.

"You think so?"

She smoothed away the lines of worry from his brow, for once aware of an air of uncertainty about him. "I'm sure of it, Jarrod. He's a strong man. He'll pull through, you'll see," she smiled bravely.

He touched her cheeks with gentle fingers. "I wish I had your optimism."

"You'll call me as soon as you know anything?" she asked anxiously.

He moved impatiently away from her, beginning to button his shirt. "It could be any time of day or night when we know he's out of danger."

"I want to know, Jarrod," she said firmly.

"Look, it can't mean that much to you." He pulled on his jacket, ready to leave. "My family are nothing to you and neither am I."

"Jarrod!" she said warningly, more hurt than she cared to admit. He had shown her very effectively that what had just taken place between them was no more than a physical attraction that was easily forgotten by him.

"Okay, okay, I'll call you."

He left the bedroom without another word and by the time she had gathered her wits together enough to follow him he and Dave had already left. She sank down dejectedly on the couch. Would she ever see Jarrod again? Tonight he had been consumed with a desire so strong it couldn't be denied, but now that passion had faded and died, and so had his desire to see her for all she knew.

She didn't bother to go back to bed, dozing on the couch until about ten o'clock when she decided she may as well shower and dress. Jarrod hadn't called her, yet, and so she waited by the telephone all day in the hope that she would hear from him.

No call came and as she hadn't thought to ask the name of the hospital Mr. Stone had been admitted to she couldn't call and inquire after his health for herself. Not that she thought they would tell her anything, anyway, she wasn't "family."

She was thoroughly exhausted by the time eleven

o'clock came around that evening, lack of sleep and loss of appetite were each paying their toll and she just had to go to bed. She would be fit for nothing in the morning, and she still had to go to work even if she was—had been, engaged to the boss.

The bed felt curiously lonely without Jarrod's presence and she found it difficult to fall asleep. When she finally did it was a deep drugged sleep from which she would find it difficult to awaken.

She woke part way through the night to find a strong masculine arm curved around her waist and a heavy weight resting on her breasts. Jarrod murmured in his sleep as she moved in surprise.

"Jarrod?" she muttered drowsily, looking down at the dark head resting against her.

"Mmm?" He didn't move.

"Is everything all right?" her fogged-up brain formed the question.

"Mmm," he said again, a smile momentarily curving his mouth.

She was satisfied with that. Jarrod wouldn't be here and he wouldn't have smiled if his father wasn't out of danger. She drifted back off to sleep, content just to have him here.

When she woke in the morning he had gone. She couldn't believe it, jumping out of bed and rushing into the bathroom to see if he was showering. He was nowhere to be found, making her wonder if she had dreamed the whole thing. Surely she hadn't imagined it? But there could be no other explanation.

She was still pale and tired when she arrived at work, her head throbbing with pain. "Don't say it," she groaned as Jean was about to speak. "I know I look terrible."

"Actually I was going to ask you if you would like a coffee."

She gave a grateful smile. "I'd love one, thank you. It might help wake me up."

Jean returned with the steaming cup of coffee. "I guess you had a lousy weekend."

Brooke swallowed a couple of aspirins. "You heard?"

"About Mr. Stone?" She nodded. "It was on the radio."

"It was terrible—such a shock." In more ways than one for Jarrod and herself!

"The boss looked in terrible shape when he came in," Jean said sympathetically.

"Jarrod's in?" she squeaked, scalding her mouth with the hot coffee.

Jean nodded. "About fifteen minutes ago."

"Oh."

"I don't think he'll be staying though," Jean continued. "He was dressed very casually," she explained. "Not his usual suave self. He's probably only in to read the mail."

"Probably." She looked up as one of the girls from the typing pool came over to her desk. "Hello, Maureen. Anything wrong?" she asked at the other girl's puzzled look.

"Well, I...." Maureen looked confused. "I thought I was supposed to be taking over for you today," she explained.

Brooke frowned. "For me? Why should you think that?" Maureen usually took over the reception desk for her if she was on holiday or off sick.

"Mr. Stone phoned to say he wouldn't be in today. I naturally assumed it was because of his father's illness."

Before Brooke could protest Jean interrupted the conversation. "I think that's an excellent idea. Why don't you go home and get some sleep, Brooke? You look as if you need it."

"Thanks!"

"Look, you know you feel lousy," Jean persisted.

It was true, she did. Her temples ached, her head was pounding and her body felt like lead. But there was really no need for Jarrod to have automatically announced she wouldn't be in today. He had no idea how she felt so that couldn't possibly have been his reason for interfering.

"Go on," Jean persuaded. "It will do..." she broke off impatiently as her intercom buzzed. "Yes? Yes, sir." She glanced at Brooke. "Right away. Goodbye." She disconnected the line. "You don't have any choice about it now. Apparently Mr. Stone has just learned you're in the building after all. He wants you to go up to his office."

Brooke would have liked to protest at this, but she was too much aware of Maureen and the gossip such objections could cause. With a shrug she gathered up her jacket and handbag and walked over to the private elevator.

Catherine Farraday, treating her with none of the haughtiness of their last meeting, smiled at her. She pressed the intercom at her side. "Your fiancée is here to see you, Mr. Stone."

"Ask her to come in." His voice sounded strangely hollow over the intercom.

"I'll show myself in, shall I?" Brooke asked tentatively.

"Certainly," she smiled again.

She knocked on the door to Jarrod's office before entering. He was sitting behind the desk and he looked as terrible as she felt. His face was deathly pale, his eyes dark and heavy from lack of sleep, and his hair was ruffled as if he had spent many hours running agitated hands through its thickness.

He was dressed just as casually as Jean had said he was, the denims fitting snugly on his hips and the matching denim shirt buttoned carelessly halfway up his chest.

He looked up at her as he sorted through the letters on his desk. "I didn't expect you to be in to work today," he said curtly.

"I gathered that," she returned dryly. "I waited all

day yesterday for you to call me," she added gently, still not sure if his father was out of danger or if things had gone drastically the other way.

He sat back with a sigh, his mind obviously not on what he was doing. "It was late last night when my father came out of the critical stage, and I didn't want to disturb you with a telephone call at two o'clock in the morning. It could have frightened you."

"I wouldn't have minded, Jarrod. I wanted to know."

His gray eyes flashed angrily. "Do you think I didn't realize that?" he snapped. "You had told me most definitely that you wanted to know, so I came around to your apartment."

A terrible trembling started in her lower limbs. "You...you did?"

"Yes," he confirmed wearily. "It must have been three o'clock by this time. You had already gone to bed. And you had foolishly left your door unlocked," he added sternly.

"I...I had?" She had a terrible feeling that her "dream" of Jarrod snuggled up against her hadn't been a dream at all, in fact she felt sure it wasn't.

"Mmm." A glimmer of a smile curved his mouth. "I, er, I let myself in."

Brooke cleared her throat in embarrassment. "Er...did you? I didn't hear you." She couldn't meet his probing eyes.

"I'm not surprised, you were fast asleep. Luckily I wasn't a burglar. As it was all I wanted was a bed for the night. You were still sleeping when I left at seven-thirty."

"I...I woke once in the night." She fidgeted with the strap of her handbag.

"Ah," he nodded understandingly. "Then there's no need for me to explain further." He resumed sorting through the mail.

"I thought I had imagined you being there."

He looked at her sharply. "Did you *want* to imagine it?"

Color flared in her cheeks. "No . . . I— But I couldn't think how you came to be in my bed—in my room."

"I told you, you left the door open," he said absently.

"It won't happen again," she muttered.

"Oh, I didn't mind. I was too tired to go home." He looked up at her. "And you do look very beautiful when you're asleep. Sleeping with you could become a habit."

"As long as it's only sleep you have in mind." She attempted to make light of it.

He gave her a long hard look. "I wouldn't guarantee it." He closed the folder containing his mail. "Right, that's done. Are you ready to leave?"

"I was going home, yes, as you seem to have made arrangements for me not to be here."

"I expected you to be sleeping in this morning."

"I still have a job to do."

"And I still happen to be the owner of this firm, and I don't consider you fit for work." He stood up. "Besides, I have plans for you today."

Her eyebrows rose. "And what plans are these?"

"My father wants to see you." He picked up the folder in preparation for leaving. "I'll just give these things to Catherine and then she can get the letters off in today's mail."

"Your father wants to see me?" She couldn't help her surprise.

"Yes." He opened the door for her. "Shall we go?"

"Yes. But I— Your father wants to see *me*?"

"I've just said so," he told her impatiently. "Let's go, Brooke. I only came in at all today to deal with the mail. I want to get back to the hospital. Dave had to be back on duty at ten o'clock this morning so my mother and Angie are at the hospital alone."

"Of course."

She followed him out to his secretary's office, standing quietly to one side as he gave her instructions for the day. It gave her a chance to look at him without being observed herself. He was his usual handsome self but the strain of the last couple of days showed in the lines etched on either side of his mouth and nose, and for the first time since she had known him he looked every one of his thirty-seven years.

Brooke's heart went out to him and she wished she could comfort him in some way. But he had made it obvious on Saturday night that he didn't want her sympathy.

They went down in the elevator together, deciding to drive their respective vehicles back to Brooke's home and carry on together in Jarrod's car from there. She parked her car before joining him.

He turned in his seat to look at her. "I noticed you're not wearing your ring. Go and get it," he ordered coldly.

She was angered by his tone. "I'm no longer engaged to you. I was going to return your ring and the other gifts, including the car, at the earliest opportunity."

He leaned his arms on the steering wheel. "Get the ring, Brooke. Our personal vendetta can wait until later. My family believes us to be still getting married."

"You haven't told them we've argued?"

He gave a taunting smile. "The weekend was hardly the time to tell them."

"I suppose not." She opened the car door to get out. "I won't be a moment."

"I didn't intend to leave without you," he returned dryly.

She didn't respond to his sarcasm. They were both under great strain and an argument between them wouldn't help matters. She got the ring from the back of the drawer she had locked it in. Not that this little lock would stop a burglar if he were really determined, but she couldn't think what else to do with it. At least she had made sure Jarrod had the other jewelry.

He looked at her hand with satisfaction as she got back in beside him, starting the car without another word.

His silence angered Brooke. "I'm only wearing this as a temporary measure," she told him stiffly. "As soon as we leave your family you can have it back."

He gave her a cold look. "You'll wear it for as long as my father can be hurt by the knowledge that the wedding is off."

"I—"

"You'll wear it, Brooke! You may be a flirt and a little cheat but for the moment I don't think it would benefit my father to know that. He likes you," he added grimly.

"I like him, too." Tears shimmered in her eyes at the reputation she had deliberately earned herself with the man she loved.

"Then do this for him if for no one else. He just isn't strong enough to take the news, he won't be for several weeks. No shocks or disappointments the doctor said." He drove the car into a hospital parking space. "And he'll be both of those things if we call off the wedding, shocked because he believes us to be genuinely in love, and disappointed because he thought I was going to settle down and give him grandchildren."

"I told you it was a mistake from the beginning to involve your family. It was bad enough that you insisted on maintaining our engagement to your friends, but—"

"I had a reason for that," he cut in abruptly, pulling his leather jacket out of the backseat.

"Oh, I know that, your arrogant pride! I'd played a trick on you and no one is allowed to get away with that," she said fiercely.

"Precisely." He got out of the car, opening her door for her. "Now, forget your tantrums and act the loving fiancée."

She shivered. "I couldn't!" How could she put on an act when it was a reality, a reality that Jarrod must never see. How easily she had nearly fallen for his charm on Saturday night, and how Jarrod would relish the added knowledge that she loved him.

His face was a shuttered mask. "Just try not to cringe when I touch you."

"I'll try," she whispered huskily.

Once inside the hospital Jarrod ordered his mother and sister back to his apartment for a shower, a change of clothes and something to eat. His mother was very reluctant to leave but Jarrod was adamant.

Brooke couldn't help but feel shocked by just how ill his father looked. His skin was gray, his eyes sunken into his head and his body almost looked shrunken. But although he looked ill the blue eyes were keen enough, his face lighting up with pleasure as he saw the two of them.

The greetings over, they sat beside his bed, Jarrod conversing easily about everyday things. Brooke listened to them silently, a slight curve to her lips for his father's benefit.

Clifford Stone turned to look at her, smiling even in his pain. "You're very quiet, Brooke," he said gently. "You mustn't let all this disturb you," he indicated the heartbeat monitor and the trolley of instruments in one corner of the room. "It's all for show."

She knew it wasn't, but she returned his smile. "I'm just glad to know you're feeling better, Mr. Stone."

"Well enough for your wedding not to be postponed next month. I may not be able to be at the actual ceremony but the reception can be held at the house, I can enjoy that."

"Oh, but—"

Jarrod's warning glare silenced her. "Don't worry, dad. We knew how you would feel about it and so we have no intention of postponing the wedding."

CHAPTER TEN

"WHAT WEDDING next month?" Brooke demanded of him.

They had arrived back at her apartment five minutes earlier, after spending an hour with Jarrod's father. Jarrod would be returning to the hospital shortly but he had made it obvious her presence wasn't needed.

"Jarrod, I said what wedding?" she repeated impatiently.

He gave a taunting smile. "Ours, of course."

"But there isn't going to be a wedding! I already told you that I have no intention of remaining engaged to you a moment longer than necessary. As for getting married!" She shook her head. "That's totally out of the question."

"You can't stand to be near me, is that it?"

"Exactly."

"Funny," he mocked her. "You gave a totally different impression Saturday night."

"That was Saturday night," she said crossly, her cheeks fiery red.

"I see. And things have changed since then, in two days?"

The cynical hardness of his eyes mocked her in that way that she found so annoying, almost as if he were secretly laughing at her—again. "Two days can sometimes seem a lifetime. And may I remind you that I wasn't engaged to you on Saturday night."

"Exactly," he repeated her word of a few minutes

earlier, but with such sarcasm that she couldn't misunderstand his implication.

She blushed again. "Meaning?"

"Meaning I wasn't engaged to you. As I wasn't last night when you snuggled into my arms as if you did it every night of your life."

"I didn't know it was you! I..." she broke off as she realized how damning that sounded.

Jarrod's mouth turned back in a sneer. "Don't incriminate yourself any further, Brooke. I already know you for what you are. And don't ask me to explain that, too."

She looked the other way. "That won't be necessary."

"I didn't think it would be."

"Your being insulting doesn't solve the problem of what we do about this expected wedding."

"Expected is all it will be. We have plenty of time to get out of it."

"You call four weeks plenty of time!" She looked skeptical. "God, the whole thing will be arranged before you can call it off. Couldn't you just tell your mother the truth? She wouldn't have to tell your father but it would save us all the embarrassment of having to cancel everything."

"You selfish little bitch! Does nothing matter to you but your own embarrassment?" he demanded fiercely. "No, of course it doesn't. Why should it matter to you that my mother is as worried as hell about my father. As long as you don't have any *embarrassment* to face you'll be happy. And that's all that matters to you, your own happiness."

"That isn't true! I—"

"Don't give me that, Brooke," he interrupted coldly. "Your actions since we first met have all been self-centered. You involved me in this engagement because you felt insulted, announced our forthcoming marriage to Selina because of a conversation you had taken exception to. You took a liking to my brother so you decided to have him, anyway, regardless of the consequences of such action among my family. Well, now you can do something for me, you can damn well behave yourself and keep your mouth shut. And you won't see Dave again until this thing has been settled."

"You can't tell me what I can or cannot do," she retorted angrily. "If I want to see Dave I will." Although she had no inclination to do any such thing. She and Dave had nothing left to say to one another.

"You'll see no one but me until I say you can."

"Why you arrogant—"

Jarrod came toward her, a determined glint in his eyes. "It seems there's only one way of silencing you." He pulled her roughly against the hard immovability of his body and she felt the first stirring of his desire against her thighs. "And if I enjoy it, too, why should I give a damn that you're nothing but a lying little cheat. Why should I give a damn!" he repeated with a groan.

His dark head bent and his mouth covered hers in utter possession. Her head was forced back and he held her immovable by one hand threaded savagely in her hair. There was no tenderness in the taking of her lips, only anger and passion and a contempt she just couldn't bear from him.

She wrenched away from him. "No, Jarrod! Stop it! I won't allow you to treat me like this."

His hold wouldn't be broken and he grinned down at her struggles with devilish satisfaction. "I'm not asking you to *allow* me to do anything," he mocked her throatily. "I'll take you any time I please." He let her go abruptly, glancing tersely at his wristwatch. "But right now I don't have the time." His eyes slid over her body with barely concealed contempt. "Or the inclination," he added dryly.

"Neither do I," she choked, rubbing her hand roughly across her mouth. "I despise you!"

"Really?" He took a threatening step forward. "Would you like me to prove differently?"

She backed away. "No...no, don't! I...I can't stand to have you near me."

His only answer was a deep mocking laugh before he turned toward the door. "I have to get back to the hospital, now, but I could be back later this evening."

"I shouldn't bother!" she snapped.

"I only said I could be. If it's late I'll—"

"You'll go home," she finished for him. "Don't expect my door to be left unlocked tonight."

He grinned. "I couldn't wish for such luck two nights running."

"I'll make sure you don't," she vowed vehemently.

Jarrod opened the door in preparation for leaving. "Don't go in to work tomorrow, I may need you during the day."

"Then you can damn well need, because I have every intention of going into work. I told you, I have a job to do."

"Okay, you're fired," he said arrogantly.

Brooke gasped. "You can't do that!"

"I know that," he agreed calmly. "But by the time you've sorted it all out my father will be out of the hospital and you can go back to work any time you want to."

"But that's not—"

"Fair?" he finished. "So, it's not fair, but it gets me what I want."

"You're a selfish—"

He grasped her arm roughly, pulling her against him with a fierce intensity. "If I'm selfish I hate to think what you are," he ground out savagely. "If my father wants to see you again I want you where I can reach you with relative ease. I don't want to have to go to the trouble of having to wait while you find yourself a replacement on the desk. Understood?"

He was shaking her so hard her teeth rattled. "Understood," she quivered.

Jarrod pushed her away so suddenly she almost fell over. "For once you aren't going to argue anymore." He shook his head. "Amazing."

"Goodbye, Jarrod," she said stiffly, her eyes violet with dislike. "I'll be here if your father asks to see me, other than that I don't want to see you."

"Try and stop me, Brooke. I still mean to take you."

She gave a choked laugh. "You have the nerve and conceit of the devil if you think that I would ever let you touch me again."

He smiled at her anger. "You can't help yourself, Brooke," he scorned. "You may keep denying it but once I touch you you don't deny it for much longer."

"Get out of here, Jarrod," she ordered, her hands clenched tightly at her side. "Just go away."

She didn't hear him move but she knew he had left, her senses told her that much. She sank down into the nearest armchair, all fight leaving her body. She couldn't go on like this much longer, she just couldn't take much more.

The most awful thing of all was that Jarrod was right, her love for him made her weak and pliant in his arms and forgetful of all the self-respect that had been inborn in her. No man who felt about her as Jarrod did should be allowed to affect her this way. He treated her as he would treat any of his casual women, Selina Howard remaining the love of his life.

She groaned. Selina Howard had a perfectly good husband of her own, a man who was charming, handsome and very rich, so why couldn't she leave Jarrod alone. Because Jarrod had a sensuous magnetism that was completely his own and would attract women all his life, that's why. Selina Howard just happened to be the woman he had given his love to, it didn't stop him wanting other women.

Brooke pummeled the cushion in the chair, angry and frustrated at the same time. She wanted Jarrod for herself, wanted and loved him, but she wouldn't have him under the conditions he wanted her, knowing that all the time Selina Howard was the woman he would go back to when her own challenge had waned. And that's all she was to Jarrod, a challenge.

The trauma of the last couple of days took its toll with Brooke and she fell asleep in the chair. The sleep was just as drugged as the night before and she felt sure that the person hammering loudly on her door must have been doing so for some time before they finally woke her.

She staggered as she stood up, pushing her wayward hair out of her eyes. A glance at her wristwatch showed her it was almost seven o'clock in the evening, and the rumblings of her stomach told her that it was high time she ate. She hadn't eaten anything substantial for two days and now felt weak with hunger. Another argument with Jarrod was the last thing she felt able to handle.

But it wasn't Jarrod standing nervously outside her door, it was his brother Dave. "Can I come in?" he asked uncertainly.

"I suppose so," she nodded dully, not feeling in the mood to be polite to him, not after what he had tried to do to her.

"Thanks." He closed the door behind him, still looking at her for some sign of softening toward him.

Brooke swayed dizzily, putting out a hand blindly to stop herself from falling. Unfortunately there was nothing to hold on to and she sank slowly to the floor in a dead faint.

She opened deeply violet eyes a few seconds later to find herself on the sofa, blinking dazedly as Dave bent over her. She attempted to sit up, sinking down against the cushions as Dave gently pushed her back down again. She smiled wanly, ashamed of her weakness.

"I'm sorry about this. I don't usually fall at the feet of my visitors."

He grinned down at her. "It's an unusual greeting I must admit, but I didn't mind. Quite nice really."

She couldn't resist his smile. "I don't know what's the matter with me. I suddenly became faint. I feel rather silly now."

He looked suddenly serious. "Have you felt like this before? Feelings of sickness, dizziness?"

She shook her head. "No. It's nothing to worry about, I—"

"Everything unusual is something to worry about. Your health isn't something to be taken lightly. There has to be a reason for you fainting. Have you..." he broke off, a ruddy hue rising in his cheeks. "Oh!" he looked embarrassed.

"Yes?"

"Well, I— It's none of my business." He turned away stiffly.

Brooke frowned. "What are you thinking now, Dave?" she sighed, sitting up but not having enough energy to stand up. "Don't bother to tell me, I can imagine what you're thinking, especially with the impression Jarrod has tried to give you of our relationship. But I'm not pregnant, I'm just hungry. Such a lot has been happening the last couple of days that I seem to have forgotten to eat."

His obvious relief showed in his face. "You mean you haven't eaten at all?"

"I've drunk a lot of coffee but had no food."

Dave threw off his jacket and rolled up the sleeves of his shirt. "Stay right there and I'll get you an omelet and a cup of strong sweet tea."

"I don't take sugar in my tea," she protested.

"This time you will," he said firmly. "Doctor's orders," he grinned.

"Jarrod warned me about you," she teased. "I thought he was joking."

"He wasn't. I take all this very seriously. Now just stay there while I get you some food."

She laughed. "I wasn't going to move. Will you be able to find everything?"

"I'll manage."

And he did—within a few minutes producing her a light fluffy omelet and the promised tea. She grimaced as she drank this, but forced it down under his watchful eye. "You certainly cook a good omelet." She sat back replete.

"It's nourishing, easy and quick to cook. It's usually all I have time for."

"You're quite amazing really. I could never imagine Jarrod being able to do anything like that." She made a face. "He told me he has a housekeeper."

"Oh, he does, but he can shift for himself like the rest of us. At my age Jarrod was just starting out in business, and like me he refused help from our father."

"I didn't realize, Jarrod always gives the impression of being...well, of being...."

"I know exactly what you mean," he sympathized. "But he was just as hard up as we are once." He took the plate from her hand. "Feeling better now?"

"Much." She smiled gratefully.

He came back from the kitchen. "I really came around to ask if you've forgiven me for the other evening. I know Jarrod's temper and I'm afraid I did nothing to allay his suspicions."

Brooke squeezed his hand reassuringly. "Well, we're still engaged." She held up her hand with the ring on that she had forgotten to remove after parting from Jarrod. "So he couldn't have been that annoyed."

"I'm glad, I'm not usually such a swine. My only excuse is that I rather like you myself." He shrugged.

"Still, I suppose I'll get used to the fact that the clos-est relationship I'll ever have with you will be as your brother-in-law." He looked at his watch. "I have to go now. I just wanted to clear things up between us."

"And prepare me a lovely meal." She stood up as he did, following him to the doorway. "It was nice of you to come around, I appreciate it."

He opened the door before turning to face her. "Can I claim a brotherly kiss?"

"As long as that's all it is—and it's only the one," she added teasingly.

The kiss couldn't exactly be called brotherly but she didn't have the heart to protest. In fact, she didn't have the chance. Dave was pulled roughly away from her, leaving her dazed as she stared up into the lividly angry face of Jarrod.

His gray eyes were like slate as he glared at his brother. "Get out of here, Dave," he ordered forci-bly. "Before I do something we'll both regret."

"Jarrod, it wasn't—"

"Get out, Dave!" Jarrod repeated through gritted teeth.

Dave gave Brooke a helpless look before leaving. She turned to reenter her apartment, realizing that Jarrod was angry beyond reason.

But he wasn't going to let her go so easily, swinging her around to face him. "Can't you stay away from my brother for just a few weeks?" he demanded coldly. "At least until my father is out of hospital. Good God, girl, are you so much in love with him that a few weeks is too much to ask?"

"I—"

"No wonder you told me not to come back here, you knew Dave was coming over. Each time I see you I become more and more disillusioned with you and yet I..." he shook his head. "I still find myself want-ing you. What do you have that makes men want you, myself, Dave, that boy, Jerry? What is it about you

that we all find so attractive?'' He looked at her criti-
cally, making her feel as if he stripped the very clothes
from her body. ''I can't see what it is, you're not as
beautiful as hundreds of other women I know.''

''Including Selina Howard,'' she put in bitchily.

''Especially the lovely Selina.''

''What did you come here for, Jarrod?'' she asked,
angry and hurt.

''My father would like to see you tomorrow. I'll call
for you about ten o'clock.''

''I'll be ready. Perhaps now you've said what you
came here to say you'll leave,'' she requested quietly,
unable to meet the disgust in his eyes. He was right,
each time they met she gave him an even worse impression of herself, mainly because of her lie that she
and Dave were in love. If he should ever ask Dave
about that love! But he never would, he wasn't that
interested in her and his pride wouldn't allow for it,
either.

''Don't worry,'' he said harshly. ''I have no intention of staying any longer than I have to. Good
night.''

After that each day progressed the same, she would
visit the hospital in the morning with Jarrod and
spend the rest of the time alone. She was pale and
growing thinner daily, but luckily Jarrod's family put
this down to the strain they were all under. Jarrod
himself hardly spoke to her and she lived in daily
dread of him telling her that this was the day their
association came to an end.

By the time Friday evening came she was in such a
state of nervous tension that any change in the routine of the last few days was welcome. Consequently
she welcomed Jerry's unexpected visit with open
arms.

Jerry looked around suspiciously. ''No fiancé this
evening?''

''Nor any other evening.''

He looked surprised. "I heard you were back together."

Brooke smiled. "And where did you hear that?" She sat opposite him, her knees tucked beneath her chin as she looked at him.

"It was in the newspapers that you and your fiancé have been visiting Clifford Stone with the rest of the family. I naturally assumed the engagement was back on."

"For the moment," she acknowledged.

"For the moment?"

"Until Mr. Stone is strong enough to take the news."

"Oh, I see. I was a bit uncertain about coming around this evening, but I'm glad I did now. I..." he broke off as the doorbell rang. "Are you expecting someone?"

She frowned. "No."

"Oh, God, I have a nasty feeling.... Does this Jarrod of yours get violent? I haven't forgotten his threat. I like you, honey, but I don't particularly want to have to fight over you."

She stood up with a laugh. "It won't be Jarrod. He never comes here now, except to take me to see his father."

The door swung open before she reached it, making a lie of her statement. Jarrod was the only one arrogant enough to walk into her home uninvited. He was dressed quite casually in black corduroys and a black silk shirt, and her heart jumped nervously at the sight of him.

"Jarrod," she said lamely.

He smiled easily, completely unlike the cold front he had been showing to her all week. His eyes narrowed slightly as Jerry came to stand beside her. "Am I interrupting anything?" he asked softly.

"No! Yes...no..." she wanted him here but she didn't want another argument. Before he had seen

Jerry there had been a softness in his gaze that she had never seen before. She looked at him sharply, a terrible feeling in the pit of her stomach. "Your father, is he—"

"He's fine," he reassured her quickly. He looked at Jerry, a charming smile lighting up his face. "I'm afraid I still don't know your name, but it's nice to meet you again, Mr....." He looked at him inquiringly.

"Saunders, Jerry Saunders," he supplied, obviously bowled over by this charm.

Jarrod shook his hand. "And I'm Jarrod Stone, but then you already know that. Actually I came over to discuss the wedding date with Brooke. Had you forgotten?" he asked her.

"I...no, I...I didn't realize it would be tonight." Her face was paler than ever. Tonight was the night Jarrod would sever their relationship once and for all. Oh, God, she couldn't live without him!

"I thought you were aware of our plans."

"Yes, but I...I just didn't realize it would be so soon."

"I can see no point in waiting any longer."

Jerry looked a little uncomfortable. "I, er, I think I'll leave, now. See you, Brooke, Mr. Stone." He nodded abruptly and left.

"What was he doing here?" Jarrod demanded once they were alone.

Brooke was taken aback at his anger, none of it having shown a few minutes earlier. "He—"

"No, don't bother to explain," he rasped. "I don't want to know."

"You said you wanted to discuss the wedding date," she reminded. "Or lack of it. Your mother telephoned this afternoon, she thinks it's time we did something about the arrangements. Is that what's made you decide to call the whole thing off?"

"But I haven't."

"Haven't what?"

"Decided to call the whole thing off. On the contrary, I think my mother has the right idea. It *is* time you did something about the arrangements. My mother will enjoy helping you."

Her eyes widened. "But I—We aren't...."

Jarrod looked amused. "Aren't what? Before you say any more I think I should tell you that I had a word with Dave today. He seemed very surprised that the two of you were supposed to be lovers. In fact, he denied it emphatically. Not that he didn't like the idea, he just knew it wasn't true. Why did you tell me it was?"

He was so tall and intimidating and she unconsciously moved away from him. "I— It seemed to be what you wanted to hear."

"Come on, Brooke," he chided gently. "You know damn well it was the last thing I wanted to hear. I've been puzzling over it ever since I spoke to Dave and I can't come up with the reason you lied to me about it."

"You can't?" Her voice was husky, her eyes wide with the fear that he had discovered her secret.

"No, I can't, but you can tell me it in a minute. First I want to tell you something, quite a lot of things in fact. I'll begin with the day we got engaged. When I found out what you'd done I was angry, furiously angry."

She smiled as she remembered that anger. "I know that. It was unmistakable."

"But that anger soon faded. I became very curious about you; you're so unlike anyone else I've ever met. You don't let me bully you for a start, which I find quite intriguing."

"I never would have thought it," she said dryly.

"No one has ever stood up to me as you do. So I became attracted to you, mindlessly so. The attraction grew so strong that I just knew I had to have you. I know I haven't always been kind, but you've given me great provocation. I'm not used to denying myself anything and you were denying me all the time. That day I kissed you in the woods adjoining my family home I had been pushed almost beyond endurance, holding you in my arms all night."

"You didn't show it. You appeared very calm and collected when you woke up the next morning." Too much so as far as she had been concerned!

"I wasn't. I escaped out of that bedroom as quickly as I could before I let you see how much I wanted to get back in bed with you and stay there all day."

"Jarrod!" She blushed scarlet.

He grimaced. "I know, I know. But I couldn't help myself, you have no idea the difficulty I had controlling myself. As it turned out I had only dampened down the passion for as long as it took me to see you again. If Dave hadn't come along and interrupted us I think I would have taken you right then. But he did interrupt us and after that I was frightened I may have scared you. You see, I'm not a boy who can be satisfied with a few kisses. I wanted everything from you. But my age has been a certain barrier between us." He scowled.

Brooke didn't know where this conversation was leading to, but this certainly wasn't the arrogant Jarrod she was used to. "Your age has never come between us. I've never even thought about it, except that it gives you a certain amount of experience I don't have."

"That I wouldn't want you to have. But it seems to me that every time I've been to see you lately I've had to throw out one young man or another," he moved impatiently. "You can't realize what it's done to me to see you with them."

She couldn't, but she knew she couldn't let him be misled about them any longer. "The only times they've been here is when you've called. It was just pure coincidence."

"That may be so, but it doesn't alter the fact that you have more in common with them than I can ever hope for you to have with me. I'm thirty-eight next month, seventeen years older than you."

"It doesn't matter," she insisted quietly.

"Of course it does," he denied violently. "But I've come here tonight to ask you to marry me, anyway."

Her eyes widened. "You're *asking* me?"

"Yes, I'm asking." His look was anxious.

She shook her head. "But I...I don't understand. You said you would make me beg for marriage," she reminded him dazedly.

"And now I'm the one doing the begging," he said bitterly. "And I am begging, Brooke."

"But...but why?"

"Why?" He gave a harsh laugh. "I've just been telling you why."

"Because you desire me. But you know I won't marry you because of that."

"I know I've been cruel and harsh and that I've accused you of things that just aren't true. I know you've never been with a man; I knew that and yet I still kept taunting you. I didn't want to feel this way about you, Brooke. But I can't help it."

"What way?"

"I love you, damn you!" he said violently, noting her shocked face. "Hard to believe, isn't it, when you consider how badly have to put my harsh behavior down to, temporary insanity." He grasped her shoulders. "But I'm sane now, sane enough to know that I love you and want to marry you. Will you have me?"

"I...I don't know what to say." She searched his face for some sign of mockery. "This isn't a trick to get me to admit to wanting you enough to marry you, is it?"

He frowned, but it wasn't an angry frown. "Oh, God, I've treated you worse than I thought. Telling you I love you isn't enough, is it? I've lost your trust, haven't I?"

"I don't know," she admitted truthfully. "It's just such a shock to hear you say you love me. You've never shown it in any way."

"I was a man in the last throes of losing the freedom I've always thought I valued above everything else, and I could be losing it to a woman who doesn't give a damn for me. You were attracted to me, I knew that, but it wasn't what I wanted. I tried so hard to make you admit to some feelings for me that in the end you retreated from me altogether. But whether you love me or not, whether you marry me or not, I'll never be free again. You have a large part of me I'll never get back, that I don't want back."

Her face softened at the look of utter defeat on his face. She touched his cheek gently, a large emotional lump rising in her throat as he turned to bury his face in her palm, his lips caressing, his eyes pleading. "There's freedom in love, too, Jarrod. A different sort of freedom, but it is freedom."

His look was hopeful. "Does that mean that you . . . that you—"

She couldn't bear his pain a moment longer. "I love you," she finished for him. "Much longer than you've loved me, ever since I came to work for you, in fact."

His eyes were almost black with passion, a look of such intense adoration on his face. He pulled her close against him, his hands molding her to the contours of his body, his sigh one of deep satisfaction. "Oh, God, Brooke," he quivered against her. "I had given up hope. I tried for so long to make you love me and you always rejected me. I thought I had alienated you forever." He looked down at her anxiously. "Do you really love me?"

She smiled at him gently. "Really."

He buried his face in her throat. "I don't deserve

this," he muttered. "But I need you so much that I don't care how I get you."

Brooke felt like crying with happiness. Jarrod loved her and wanted to marry her. Nothing else mattered anymore, not the bitterness or the misunderstandings. "Kiss me, Jarrod," she pleaded. "I promise I won't reject you this time." Or ever again! They lay on the sofa, their arms around each other as they mused over the fact that they had loved each other for weeks and neither of them had realized it.

Suddenly Brooke sat up with a jerk, her face paling. "Selina Howard," was the only explanation she gave to his worried expression.

He pulled her back down to rest her head on his shoulder. "Forget her."

"But you . . . you love her."

He laughed softly. "Of course, I don't. I love you, I thought I had just proved that . . . very effectively," he added with remembered satisfaction.

"But all this time— You said you were having an affair with her, that you loved her," she insisted with remembered pain.

"Correction, *you* said those things. I just played along with you."

"But why did you do that?"

"Because in the beginning, before I began to fall for you, I kept up our engagement to punish you. You've been right about me all along, I'm a selfish swine where women are concerned. And I didn't like the fact that one of them had got back at me. I didn't intend for it to last long, just long enough to put you through hell," he admitted. "But at Philip's party when you accused me of being Selina's lover I saw red. I was determined to make you suffer. I let you believe those lies about Selina and myself because I knew my denying them wouldn't help, you wouldn't have believed me."

"You could have tried to explain," she pouted.

Jarrod bent his head to kiss her. "I could have, but then I realized I needed a good excuse to keep the engagement going, you weren't going to be fooled by the 'having to keep it up for show' story. After I kissed you at my parents' house I knew that for the first time in my life I was in love; that I wanted a woman so badly I had to marry her. But I'm afraid patience has never been my strong point and I tried to seduce you into marrying me. When that failed I lost my temper and started accusing you of having affairs with every man you came into contact with."

"I noticed."

"It was a form of defense," he insisted. "But I have never had an affair with Selina and I certainly don't love her. I may have been a bit of a rogue in the past but I have never had an affair with a married woman."

"But everyone said—"

"Everyone *thought* they knew, but they were all wrong. Now kiss me, woman, and stop saying ridiculous things."

She went into his arms with renewed eagerness, holding nothing back as she showed him just how much she loved him. He was pale and strained by the time he pulled reluctantly away from her, buttoning his shirt with shaking hands.

"I have to leave now before I forget how innocent you really are," he said grimly. "I haven't forgotten how you once accused me of being the type of man to take advantage of the engagement and forget about the wedding."

Brooke stilled his movements. "Stay with me tonight."

He shook his head firmly, standing up to tuck his shirt back into the waistband of his corduroys. "I can wait until we're married. Never let it be said I seduced you into marrying me."

She moved to stand in front of him. "I would never

say that. I was angry when I made that comment about forgetting the wedding. Please, Jarrod, stay with me."

"No. I respect and love you too much to do that. That's what makes you so special to me, Brooke, the fact that I may want you like hell, but I can wait until I have my ring firmly on your finger."

Tears gathered at his words. "Oh, Jarrod."

"Don't tempt me, woman," he growled. "Just make the wedding soon, I don't have much self-control left where you're concerned."

She stood on tiptoe to kiss him. "As soon as possible," she promised.

"Tomorrow?" he asked hopefully.

"If you like."

They laughed together, completely confident in their love for each other.

Let Your Imagination Fly Sweepstakes

Rules and Regulations:

NO PURCHASE NECESSARY

1. Enter the Let Your Imagination Fly Sweepstakes 1, 2 or 3 as often as you wish. Mail each entry form separately bearing sufficient postage. Specify the sweepstake you wish to enter on the outside of the envelope. Mail a completed entry form or, your name, address, and telephone number printed on a plain 3"x 5" piece of paper to:

HARLEQUIN LET YOUR IMAGINATION FLY SWEEPSTAKES,
P.O. BOX 1280, MEDFORD, N.Y. 11763 U.S.A.

2. Each completed entry form must be accompanied by 1 Let Your Imagination Fly proof-of-purchase seal from the back inside cover of specially marked Let Your Imagination Fly Harlequin books (or the words "Let Your Imagination Fly" printed on a plain 3"x 5" piece of paper. Specify by number the Sweepstakes you are entering on the outside of the envelope.

3. The prize structure for each sweepstake is as follows:

Sweepstake 1 - North America

Grand Prize winner's choice: a one-week trip for two to either Bermuda; Montreal, Canada; or San Francisco. 3 Grand Prizes will be awarded (min. approx. retail value $1,375. U.S., based on Chicago departure) and 4,000 First Prizes: scarves by nik nik, worth $14. U.S. each. All prizes will be awarded.

Sweepstake 2 - Caribbean

Grand Prize winner's choice: a one-week trip for two to either Nassau, Bahamas; San Juan, Puerto Rico; or St. Thomas, Virgin Islands. 3 Grand Prizes will be awarded. (Min. approx. retail value $1,650. U.S., based on Chicago departure) and 4,000 First Prizes: simulated diamond pendants by Kenneth Jay Lane, worth $15. U.S. each. All prizes will be awarded.

Sweepstake 3 - Europe

Grand Prize winner's choice: a one-week trip for two to either London, England; Frankfurt, Germany; Paris, France; or Rome, Italy. 3 Grand Prizes will be awarded. (Min. approx. retail value $2,800. U.S., based on Chicago departure) and 4,000 First Prizes: 1/2 oz. bottles of perfume, BLAZER by Anne Klein. (Retail value over $30. U.S.). All prizes will be awarded.

Grand trip prizes will include coach round-trip airfare for two persons from the nearest commercial airport serviced by Delta Air Lines to the city as designated in the prize, double occupancy accommodation at a first-class or medium hotel, depending on vacation, and $500. U.S. spending money. Departure taxes, visas, passports, ground transportation to and from airports will be the responsibility of the winners.

4. To be eligible, Sweepstakes entries must be received as follows:

Sweepstake 1 Entries received by February 28, 1981
Sweepstake 2 Entries received by April 30, 1981
Sweepstake 3 Entries received by June 30, 1981
Make sure you enter each Sweepstake separately since entries will not be carried forward from one Sweepstake to the next.

The odds of winning will be determined by the number of entries received in each of the three sweepstakes. Canadian residents, in order to win any prize, will be required to first correctly answer a time-limited skill-testing question, to be posed by telephone, at a mutually convenient time.

5. Random selections to determine Sweepstake 1, 2 or 3 winners will be conducted by Lee Krost Associates, an independent judging organization whose decisions are final. Only one prize per family, per sweepstake. Prizes are non-transferable and non-refundable and no substitutions will be allowed. Winners will be responsible for any applicable federal, state and local taxes. Trips must be taken during normal tour periods before June 30, 1982. Reservations will be on a space-available basis. Airline tickets are non-transferable, non-refundable and non-redeemable for cash.

6. The Let Your Imagination Fly Sweepstakes is open to all residents of the United States of America and Canada, (excluding the Province of Quebec) except employees and their immediate families of Harlequin Enterprises Ltd., its advertising agencies, Marketing & Promotion Group Canada Ltd. and Lee Krost Associates, Inc., the independent judging company. Winners may be required to furnish proof of eligibility. Void wherever prohibited or restricted by law. All federal, state, provincial and local laws apply.

7. For a list of trip winners, send a stamped, self-addressed envelope to:

Harlequin Trip Winners List, P.O. Box 1401, MEDFORD, N.Y. 11763 U.S.A.

Winners lists will be available after the last sweepstake has been conducted and winners determined. NO PURCHASE NECESSARY.

Let Your Imagination Fly Sweepstakes

OFFICIAL ENTRY FORM

Please enter me in Sweepstake No. _____

Please print:

Name _____

Address _____

Apt. No. _____ City _____

State/ _____ Zip/Postal
Prov. Code

Telephone No. area code
( )

MAIL TO:
HARLEQUIN LET YOUR
IMAGINATION FLY SWEEPSTAKE No. _____
P.O. BOX 1280,
MEDFORD, N.Y. 11763 U.S.A.

(Please specify by number, the Sweepstake you are entering.)